Beginnings

BEGINNINGS

Dorothy Livesay

1988
Peguis Publishers Limited
Winnipeg, Canada

This book is an expanded edition of *A Winnipeg Childhood,* originally published by Peguis in 1973.

Canadian Cataloguing in Publication Data
Livesay, Dorothy, 1909-
    Beginnings

    Rev. ed.--
First edition published 1973 under title: A Winnipeg childhood.
ISBN: 0-920541-94-1 :
I. Title. II. Title: A Winnipeg childhood.
PS8523.I8W5 1988   C813'.52   C88-098182-2
PR9199.3.L56W5 1988

Acknowledgement: The back-cover quote is
from Lee Briscoe Thompson's *Dorothy Livesay,*
copyright 1987, reprinted with the permission
of Twayne Publishers, a division of G.K. Hall
& Co., Boston.

Cover illustration by Scott Barham, Winnipeg
(Commissioned original, acrylic on board, 20 x 24)

Printed in Canada by
Hignell Printing Limited

ISOLATE

To find direction
the only child creates a web of action
pulling them in, to play
new, unknown games
making herself a centre

And everyday
she thinks of a new way
of charming them: some twist
to *Hide and Seek* they'd never thought of
some long manoeuvre of the map
of *Hoist Your Sails*!—called "Oyster Sales!"
And finishes, on Saturdays
holding them all intent
in half-pint chairs on the dish-towel lawn
chalking sums on a child's blackboard.

Then thunder breaks:
across the street
the firebell clangs
and the grey horses stamp
in a burst of doors
deafen the asphalt with their hooves.
Games fall apart
as children fly like sparks
with whoops and shouts
into the charging street.

She stands alone at the gate:
games fall apart.

from *Collected Poems*: The Two Seasons

Books By Dorothy Livesay

Green Pitcher, Toronto: Macmillan of Canada, 1928
Signpost, Toronto: Macmillan of Canada, 1922
Day and Night, Toronto: Ryerson Press, 1944
Poems for People, Toronto: Ryerson Press, 1947
Call My People Home, Toronto: Ryerson Press, 1950
New Poems, Toronto: Emblem Books, 1955
Selected Poems of Dorothy Livesay, The, Toronto: Ryerson Press, 1957
The Colour of God's Face, Vancouver: Unitarian Church, 1964
The Unquiet Bed, Toronto: Ryerson Press, 1967
The Documentaries, Toronto: Ryerson Press, 1968
Plainsongs, Fredericton, N.B.: Fiddlehead Poetry Books, 1969, 1971
Disasters of the Sun, Burnaby, B.C.: Blackfish, 1971
Collected Poems, The Two Seasons, Toronto: McGraw-Hill Ryerson, 1972
Nine Poems of Farewell, Windsor, Ontario: Black Moss, 1973
A Winnipeg Childhood, Winnipeg: Peguis Publishers, 1973
Ice Age, Erin, Ontario: Press Porcepic, 1975
Beginnings: A Winnipeg Childhood, (originally published as *A Winnipeg Childhood*), Toronto: New Press, 1976
Right Hand Left Hand, Erin, Ontario: Press Porcepic, 1977
The Raw Edges: Voices From our Time, Winnipeg: Turnstone Press, 1981
The Phases of Love, Toronto: Coach House, 1983
Feeling the Worlds, Fredericton, N.B.: Fiddlehead Poetry Books, 1984
Beyond War: The Poetry, Vancouver: Private printing, 1985
The Self-Completing Tree, Erin, Ontario: Press Porcepic, 1986
Beginnings, (A revised edition of *A Winnipeg Childhood,* 1973), Winnipeg: Peguis Publishers, 1988

Contents

Foreword

This collection of short stories was written by Dorothy Livesay in the fifties and sixties and was published in 1973 as *A Winnipeg Childhood.*

It has been too long out of print. Very few copies were published in the first edition and a later reprint (1976) by New Press, Toronto, was largely — inadvertantly — destroyed.

Most of the stories have appeared elsewhere, singly, in journals or collections. Together they are, as Lee Briscoe Thompson has written in her book *Dorothy Livesay,* ''a multi faceted prose poem...The language is liltingly simple and straight forward...The directness is resonant, and the sensate details of daily life viewed from a height of three feet are rendered in a way that implies their inherent mystery.''

Dorothy Livesay has written that the book is ''essentially autobiographical, and as such, represents volume I of my memoirs. Volume II is *Right Hand, Left Hand,* and Volume III, tentatively titled *Journey With Myselves,* is now being edited.''

Although no longer a "literary publisher," Peguis is pleased to offer this collection, expanded by the addition of two stories, "Good-bye Daddy" and "The Initiation." Dorothy Livesay's enthusiasm in this endeavour has been very much appreciated, and I would also like to thank Pat Sanders of Turnstone Press, Winnipeg, for her advice and cooperation. Finally I would like to acknowledge the foresight of the late Mary Scorer, founder of Peguis, for publishing the book in the first place.

Mary Dixon, Publisher,
Winnipeg, October, 1988

Preludes

There were seven houses, each one larger than the last. Like the first box in a Chinese game, you could not be sure how it was going to fit in with the others. Only at the end would you see the symmetry of the whole. Only at the end would you see the years from infancy to maturity fitting into many parts, each one larger than the last, each one branching into a new garden.

Her father's first house began the experiment. A beginning only, it had its roots far back in the past. It was a seedling from other houses he had known in England, in Ireland, in Ontario.

Elizabeth could remember it only dimly: a narrow pumpkin-coloured house with a sharply pointed roof, quite unlike the square, two-storied wooden houses with their glassed-in verandahs, so uniformly built in Winnipeg during the real estate boom of 1910-1914. This house, moreover, had not been stripped of its original trees. A grove of young oaks sheltered even its roof.

So the youngish English newspaperman and his Canadian wife, settling down to married life, must have found the little house not merely by chance: its distinctiveness must have captured them.

For Elizabeth the house would always have a blurred quality, as if shrouded in mist; as if her infant eyes had not yet focussed and people loomed huge and dark, shadows from the oak trees. Parents were wraith-like creatures who behaved unpredictably and to whom she did not belong. The only room clearly remembered in that house was upstairs, at the back, "Daddy's room". To reach it she had to go along the hall, open the door, and then down two stairs. A pale green rug covered the floor, smelling of dust, its pattern of woven green leaves nearly faded out. She must have sat long on that floor, staring at the pattern; for she was only sent to that room for mother's reasons, linked with the words "mustn't touch".

A few incidents stood out clearly. It was night. A shivering winter wind knocked rusty oak branches against the wooden walls of the house. She ran into the front room and hid her face in the black folds of a serge skirt—her mother's. "Man came," she whispered. "Bad man." Would he catch her, and carry her off? Where was the policeman who used to walk up and down the streets in his blue helmet? Was he also to be feared?

Elizabeth's hair was stroked. She was told it was just a dream. But the dream persisted. Long afterwards she was to wake up, sweating, having dreamed of those back stairs; of being trapped in that kitchen, pounding at the pantry window, her face reflected in the glass of the cupboard doors. And the feeling, so powerful, of burglars about, a nameless giant in pursuit. Was it only the fairy stories, or the gossiping servant girl, Emma? Or had it really happened? Had the terror come?

II

Those cloudy dreams vanished far into the distance when she was visiting her grandmother. Granny, mother's mother, lived only a few blocks away. Elizabeth had to cross through the huge school yard, roaring with big boys, running fast as fast for fear the fists would hit her, the legs trip her; and scutter across the road into the safety of Granny's garden.

How good it felt to hear the latch of the green gate click behind. And there was the dappled Manitoba maple, shady as a parasol; and a flower bed right near the gate with its feathery bush of "Old Man". Just to take a fistful of that bush and squeeze in her hand was joy, the scent was so strong, so musty-sweet. Granny had mignonette too, not unlike the smell of "Old Man"; and dark red sweet william, a flower so like a person, and blue bachelor buttons. There were always geraniums, set out in pots, with their own flaming red petals and their touch like velvet. Geranium leaves had a muddy smell, especially when Elizabeth was watering them from Granny's green watering-can. In deep summer she was taught how to pick the biggest poppies, turn their skirts over and tie them with a grass blade around the middle—a shining green sash. Gay dancing ladies the poppies were, whispering stories when the wind blew.

It was into the centre of this world that Granny's words fell one morning, a morning after Elizabeth had stayed overnight.

"Come, Elizabeth, there's good news. We are going over to see your Mummy now."

"Is Mummy better?"

"Yes, and I expect she will soon be able to get out of bed. And when we go over there this morning there will be such a surprise waiting for you, Elizabeth!"

A surprise! A doll, would it be a doll?

"Just imagine, your mother has found you a little baby sister!"

A baby sister. She couldn't think what that meant. It must be something important, strange. Walking across the school yard she clutched Granny's hand. The nice thing about Granny was her size. She had once been like a grown-up, but her back was bent from hard work on the farm. Now she was thin and spry, and no higher than those girls in grade six. Only her clothes weren't school clothes, but stiff and black, a shiny poplin skirt reaching down to her high-laced boots. She wore a round black straw hat, shaped like an Easter basket with a scary beetle-headed hatpin sticking out of it. As Elizabeth hopped along beside her, Granny seemed to hop, too, a tiny black ant with mild blue eyes behind gold-rimmed spectacles.

They came out of the schoolyard onto Inkster Boulevard, then to Elizabeth's street. There was the orange house, shrinking back amongst the oak trees. Elizabeth hadn't seen her mother for a few days, so she ran ahead of Granny, in through the screen door and up the stairs.

"Hello, dear!" called Mother. "Come and see what I've got!" And there, in Mother's wide bed, where *she* used to snuggle, was a round bundle with a red puckered face poking out of it. Elizabeth took it in, fast; and then hung back, uncertain.

"You can come and look at her, dear." Mother's wavy black hair covered the pillow. Her eyes were blue as Granny's bachelor buttons. "See, it's a baby sister for you to play with." That tight-blanketed bundle—to play with? Why, she wasn't even pretty, not like a doll. Elizabeth moved around gingerly to the other side of the bed.

"Jump in, beside Mummy." She did so, obediently. But lying close beside mother she felt scared even to breathe. Mother's flannelette nightgown had a sweetish, musty smell; mother's breasts were swollen and warm, hot. She lay rigid beside them.

Mother was talking of how she would soon be up and around and they would be able to go out for walks, pushing the baby carriage. She scarcely heard her mother's voice, feeling the feel of that bundle on the other side of her mother.

"Can I get up?"

"If you want to go and play now. Emma's in the kitchen. And tell Granny to come up and see me . . . . she was here, last night, when the baby came."

Elizabeth ran downstairs fast, not daring to dart another glance at the mother and baby cupped together in the wide bed. From that day on Susie, the baby, always slept there; and Elizabeth never again disturbed her by snuggling alongside.

She was three years old now; and she began to live a life outside her father's house, in the garden, in the street.

III

The drama of Winnipeg is in its seasons, its weather. The city cannot rely on mountains or hills, even, for variety; nothing but the endless flatness of prairie grass surrounds it, there where the streets end. Especially in its early sprawling days the city could not rely on trees for shade, except along the low wooded slopes of the Red River or the Assiniboine. In the raw young neighbourhoods newly planted elms, oaks, and maples struggled to grow window-high; evergreens were rare. But summer, with its intense heat, all-powerful sun, ever deepening blue sky and the long, cool twilights lasting nearly to midnight, summer pulled the child into its drama. Nights might be lit by the aurora borealis drawing, with phosphorescent fingers, vast designs upon the heavens. Or, at evening, the intolerable blanket of heat would suddenly be broken by gusts of wind, tearing up dust and leaves. Clouds would loom on the horizon in purple and black formations, rumbling with thunder; until loud as fireworks the rain would explode, great curtains of it ripped open by forked lightning; and down the barren asphalt road a pelting river of rain would sweep dust and leaves into the gutters.

"Ah-h. That'll clear the air. A wonderful storm. Come out onto the verandah and watch it!" Elizabeth, half frightened, half catching father's excitement, flattened herself against the open doorway to look at this lashing of the pavement, this agony of twisted trees, this rush for shelter by anyone caught unawares (umbrellas turned inside out on the first gust). Then, with her father, she had to burst out laughing as a Model-T Ford, dashing for home, was caught up in the storm, its top nearly ripped off but still swaying on up the roadway towards Portage Avenue, with the black, flapping canvas lifting it along. "Like a sail! like a sail!" father cried, remembering his seaside days on the Isle of Wight. But Elizabeth had never seen a sail.

That must have been their first summer in the second house, in the west end, on Lipton Street. Perhaps because it stood on a corner with unobstructed view two ways, and kitty-corner to the red brick firehall, the champing grey horses stabled mysteriously in its depths, perhaps its very geography made the white clapboard house seem much bigger than the house where she was born. This lot was bordered on two sides with a wooden sidewalk, fresh golden planks smelling of the sawmill. But father could scarcely wait to fence in the lot so that he could plant undisturbed his old-fashioned flowers—poppy, bachelor button, sweet william, and masses of portulaca and nasturtium. That left little room in front for playing space, so Elizabeth and the toddler, Susie, spent more of their time in the back vegetable garden where there was a sandbox and a swing. And before the second winter came father had rigged up a slide of old planks—a wide winter slide on which pails of water were poured, only to freeze instantly into a glass mirror. On frosty days kindergarten children peered through the gate longingly, to watch Elizabeth and Susie whizz down their slide on old tin trays.

The long months of cold were never a reason for staying inside for long. Tired of themselves, of indoor play, they would ask Katrina to help bundle them up with thick red overstockings, leggings, moccasins, a toque (they called it "tuque") for the head, a flying wool scarf with tassels and even, on the coldest day, a white veil made of soft wool mesh that covered eyes, nose and mouth. Thus secure as two red and blue woollen balls, they were tossed out into the snow to make the best of the blinding white world, the streaming sun; until mitts were fists of icicles and toes screamed with pain. Then they would come banging on the back door, lunge into the thick dark air of the kitchen, huddle around the Quebec heater in the playroom. At that, Katrina (from Austria), or it might be Marusia (from the Ukraine), would throw up her hands, rush with newspapers, as they cast down their matted mitts, pulled at the moccasin laces now sealed with ice, and cried out again for dry socks and warmer gloves. Then suddenly blissful, warm and dry again, they would plunge outdoors for another half-hour of sliding or fort-building.

After the high excitement of a winter day what Elizabeth liked best was to lie on the bear rug in front of the hall fireplace, blowing with its blue gas flames, and look at a picture book until a stamping of feet, a stamping away of snow on the verandah would indicate father's return from the office. He, whom they were afraid to speak to in the morning as he ate toast and marmalade alone, with eyes only on his newspaper, at night would return a magically different person.

As soon as his coonskin coat was off and hung on a hook in the hallway, as soon as his felt overshoes were off and Elizabeth had brought him his slippers, he was ready for fun; for tossing Susie high in his arms, then pretending to be "Big Bear" and chasing her all over the house; or, when they followed him upstairs, throwing them down on his bed for a tickle till they screamed with false pain.

Father's room in this, his second house, was not frightening, not a place of punishment. But it wasn't warm and it wasn't pretty. The narrow black iron bedstead had a loop design at the head and foot that made it seem part of an iron gate. The iron of it had a "mean" feel also, if you were turning somersaults ("wintersaults", Elizabeth called them) and your head landed too near the rail. The bed itself had no counterpane, only a bright red Hudson's Bay blanket, warmly cheerful. Beside the bed was a "whatnot" for putting pipe, tobacco and a paper called *The Times Literary Supplement*. There was just one piece of furniture that Elizabeth really liked: father's chest of drawers, of dark reddish shining wood. "Walnut," father said, "from a walnut tree." "I had a little nut tree" Elizabeth began to sing; then she asked if she might peek in the drawers, to smell the smell of tobacco, Pear's soap and stiffly laundered shirts. The ties and handkerchiefs were always in perfect order, the shirts piled neatly. So different from mother's bureau drawer, with its tangle of handkerchiefs, little bottles, salves and orange sticks.

On the walls hung father's special "finds" from a second-hand bookstore: black and white "prints". A wild boar coming out of a forest; a man's head, "Socrates". And finally father had brought upstairs others of his favourites that mother disliked having in the dining room: large "steel engravings" he called them, of two Roman gods, "Jove and Juno". They were strange bulky kind of people, Elizabeth thought, with no clothes on, only a kind of sheet draped over them. Elizabeth never looked at them too closely when there was anybody around. But she took longer looks, coming in on tiptoe at noontimes.

There was one more piece of furniture in father's bare room; placed there only because there was nowhere else to put it. A doll's house! The children had known about its making well before Christmas, because father could not hide the fact that he was spending his evenings "down cellar", hammering, sawing and swearing. Every morning the children would be allowed to go down and peek at the progress made—real glass in the tiny windows, real wallpaper, a carved fireplace, a winding stair. Of course all this had to be done before the roof was on. Elizabeth was allowed to stay up Christmas Eve to watch the completed doll's house hoisted up the cellar stairs. But there, at the door, it stuck. The roof with its overhanging eaves, so gaily painted red, was too big! The shouts and curses sent Elizabeth crying to bed.

In the end, of course, the doll's house was whole again and safely installed upstairs in father's room. Perhaps that was what gave it the feeling of being a very special place to kneel down in front of, like in church; away from all the noises of the house. Just a bare, cool floor; an iron bed; and a doll's house made by father's hands. Not to forget that naked man, Jove, hanging above her on the wall.

And Elizabeth knew these things, without being able to say them. She knew the confines of the house, and the garden around it. But she knew very little about the street and nothing of what lay at the end of it. Until one day—her fifth spring, was it?—when father called, on a Saturday morning, "Five cents for the first crocus!" They were going by streetcar to Deer Lodge to walk through prairie fields "out in the country".

IV

On that day mother stayed home, so they had father to themselves.

It was a windy day with light clouds buzzing across the blue sky; the first butterflies, pale as milk, fluttered this way and that, not sure where to go. Only a little while ago the layers of tired snow had sunk lower and lower as the sun sucked them. Icicles, streaked with dirt, would crunch in your hands, and trickle away. The sound in the streets was of water running and gurgling, of shovels hacking away at the ice; and far overhead the loud party talk of the crows. And out in the country they found that the fields were still brown. Yet after walking on snow all the long winter it was good to feel the dried grass like a cushion under their feet, springing back and rustling. It must be alive with small things like gophers and beetles. And the smell of it! That prairie grass unrolling under the wind changed Elizabeth after one whiff into a different creature, a drunken young colt snuffing up the earthy scent. Susie tried to catch her and they both fell down, rolling and rolling into the sweet turf.

"Ha, Ha!" Daddy picked them up, one after the other. He tossed Susie in the air, still kicking, her sailor hat all awry. Then as he set her down he repeated the magic words: "Five cents for the first crocus!"

With a whoop they scattered apart, bending down here and there and everywhere, looking for mauve cups hidden in the brown grass. She was dizzy with it, her eyes smarted. Was it too early? She stood erect, breathed deeply of the blue sky, the clouds scudding, the crows cawing. No, it was spring. There must be crocuses.

"I got it, I got it!" It was Susie, the baby, who found the crocus this year. Father was delighted, fished a nickel from his pocket. "Good!" And there's a whole clump of them for you, Liz. Look! Pick away then, so there are plenty to take home to mother."

She knelt down in the grass, cupped her face and held it down there amongst the mauve for a few seconds. No scent, except a fresh earth scent that seemed familiar as her own body. And how cool the petals were, how tiny the veins. But the outside cup, holding the flower, was soft and furry like a caterpillar. She picked and picked. When they had each one gathered a rounded bouquet, father tumbled the crocuses into a paper bag. The children rushed off, running towards a hayrick they saw in the distance.

They were city children, cautious of dogs. As no one was in sight, they made for the haystack, climbed on top, and slid down with a fine swish. Then up again, down again. Susie kept tumbling over herself, uttering little hoots of joy. Elizabeth began to laugh and laugh, hurling herself down on her stomach, head first, her reefer coat all prickly with hay, her sailor cap off, her unkempt hair blowing like a mop in the wind. Far off was father, standing in the field with his camera, taking cloud pictures. Suddenly he put down his camera and stood perfectly still, staring at the sky. Then Elizabeth heard it, over her head: the strange wave of sound, like a battle cry, "Honk! Honk! Honk!"

"Daddy-y-y! What's that?" she called.

"Look up, look up!" he commanded. They bent their heads back, chins tilted up like noses. There in a great "V" marching through the sky like herald angels, came the geese!

That was the first time she really lifted herself up from the earth, and saw the sky itself: a wide blue sky extending over the prairie like a winged bird, dropping soft feathers of light into the horizon. She saw the horizon! From that day onward she had a different feeling about father's house—the small white clapboard house, the stained brown rails of the fence, the wooden planks of the sidewalk—these were like fetters, holding her down. Her two hands soared, longing to sweep them away, longing to take off and break forth, free where there was only earth and sky, and a race of geese going north.

Matt

When first she started going to kindergarten Elizabeth would come home for lunch, stand beside her chair, and refuse to sit. Instead she began to scream. Her mother and Dora fluttered around her like birds, swooping and pecking. They could not quiet her.

"But what is the matter, child? Tell me what is the matter?" She did not know how to say it. Perhaps gradually she quietened, was persuaded to sit down, and then began the process of stuffing forkfuls of potato into a mouth already feeling thick and salty.

It was not as if she refused to go to kindergarten in the morning. She was a dutiful child, and whatever was pre-arranged by grown-ups she accepted as inevitable, just as God arranged the sunshine to soak through her blind in the morning. So brushed, and mouth wiped, wearing a clean striped pinafore, she made her way out into autumn, carefully memorizing ahead of time the correct route to take. Down the block towards Happyland, look to the right and left, dash across the street and walk down towards the Assiniboine River. Other children joined her but to their careless "hellos" she replied stiffly a muffled "'lo." She did not know them very well. And she had to keep an eye out for the opposite side of the street, to make sure she was early and well ahead of Matt. He arrived usually just as they were standing up to sing the morning hymn. His mother would open the playroom door and, with a quick push, send him reeling to his chair.

Fortunately, he was not at her table. And the early morning routine was something she yearned for eagerly, taking out the coloured strips of paper, so glossy, the bright sky-blue ones and the deep red like blood, combining them together to make a mat. Or else it would be raffia work, weaving real little mats and baskets to take home to mother. Her hands were slow and awkward, she was never finished when the others were. But her hands touched the square of paper, patted it, smoothed it down. "There," she said to herself, the way Dora said it when she had put a cake in the oven.

Then the moment came. The teacher clapped her hands and the children had to put everything away quickly, quickly, and push their chairs in, run to the centre of the room and form a circle. Elizabeth looked around for the little girl with the red dots on her dress and grabbed her hand. Hot and sticky it was, but preferable to any boy's hand, especially Matt's. The piano started up, and they began moving and singing, "The Farmer's in the Dell". That was nice, and so was "Ring-around-a-Rosie". But next, with panic, she heard the piano sounding the tune: "Go-In-and-Out-the-Window". In that game the children would get all mixed up, she would have to grab anyone's hand, anyone who came along.

Quickly she held her right arm up, used the left one to press the front of her dress significantly, and then she wiggled from one foot to the other. Teacher finally saw her. "All right, Elizabeth, you can surely wait till the game is over." Her hands fell numb to her sides. She hadn't really needed "to go" at all. Now she did, now she couldn't wait. Did the teacher want her to wet all over, like Ruthie?

But she didn't wet. She was pushed around, handed from child to child as the game moved along; in the bustle she hadn't time to think.

But when the game ended, there she was, just like yesterday, standing right beside Matt.

The chords of the piano banged out like a battle. As the children began to move around again in a circle, Matt seized her hand. She wanted to scream, to yank herself away, never again to feel that lumpy, clammy hand gripping hers like a sponge. She did not dare look at Matt, his leering red face cocked on one shoulder, his open mouth drooling. She tried to look the other way, at the little girl ahead, tossing brown curls. But Matt yanked her this way and that and suddenly unable to stay another moment, she pulled away her hand as if it had been stung, and ran for the door.

"Elizabeth!" But she did not heed. Teacher let her go. She ran into the dark hall and down to the end, to the bathroom.

Her trouble went on for days, weeks. She could tell no one. How could you explain that you liked kindergarten, yes, but you were terrified of holding a little boy's hand? To grown-ups, she supposed, Matt was just a little boy like anyone else, but to her, merely the sight of him made her feel sick. Then she began to notice what Matt was like when he played in the street. He would come round the corner from his street, the kindergarten street, and past the apartment house. If the big boys weren't home from school yet he would stand in the lane that ran between Elizabeth's house and the apartment block. "Y-a-aw," Matt would roar, tilting his heavy head backward as he squinted up at one of the windows. Sometimes the window would open, and a woman would stick her head out.

"Well, if it isn't Matt here again—waiting to be fed. How are you today, kid?" Matt would bellow again, the lady would break into a loud laugh and talk to someone in the apartment; then she would throw Matt a bun. The game was, he had to catch it in his teeth as it fell. If he caught it, he got another one. If he missed, he would grunt and fumble on the dirty lane for the runaway bun. "That's all for today, Matt," the woman would shout at him.

Elizabeth watched, fascinated, from the safety of her back p o r c h.

Then, with a clang of iron hoops, a loud ringing of bicycle bells, the older boys would swoop onto the corner opposite the firehall. There they began their strange boy-games of marbles, or baseball, or tag.

It was in playing tag that Matt always got caught up in the melee. "Matt's 'It', Matt's 'It'," the boys would shout in high glee. Matt would lunge, only to run and trip as he tried to catch boy after boy. When he was down they would kick him in the pants; then pull him to his feet and start all over again. "Here I am, here I am, Matt, catch me!" An imp would dance just out of Matt's reach, and Matt would begin to roar, his face crimson, his twisted, drooping mouth forming bubbles in his rage.

"Matt, Matt, the great big sap," a boy cried. Others took it up. They slapped themselves with joy, or rolled over and over in a heap, hitting and scuffling between their laughter. Eventually they would tire of the game and go off to another corner, leave Matt alone to sit sulking and wrathful on the curbstone, licking his wounds.

One such day Elizabeth ventured outside the backyard, pushing the empty garbage pail aside as she closed the gate. She began to skip up and down, up and down the wooden sidewalk. Matt was sitting on the other side of the boulevard grass, right by the road. He looked at her stupidly. His eyelids were puffy, his eyes red and rolling in his head like marbles. She skipped right on, afraid of him, yet secure in the feel of her skipping rope. And when she felt safe, even for a moment, another feeling welled in her, a feeling that *she* was sitting on the curb alone and abandoned, a child whom no one would play with. Whenever she skipped too near to him though, that tender feeling vanished: she saw only his stumpy red hands, clawing the air. Faster she skipped, whirring past him. The rhythm of her skipping seemed to take on the rhythm of those words she had heard before:

"Matt, Matt, the great big sap—"

"Matt, Matt—" she started softly. Then each time she passed him the words seemed to fall naturally out of her mouth, more loud, more daring.

"Matt, Matt, the great big sap, doesn't know how to turn a tap."

"Gimme."

She whirled around. Matt was beside her.

"Go away! Go away!" she shrilled. She shook her skipping rope at him.

"Gimme." That stubby red paw reached out, grabbed the rope.

"That's my rope. You can't have it. Go away. This is my sidewalk."

"G-r-aw." Matt was beginning to make those noises. He still held the rope, tugging and tugging. Elizabeth pulled the other way, screaming to him to go. Then the rope snapped. A handle came off in Matt's hand and he reeled backward, to the ground. She stood over him then, waving her rope.

"Now see what you've done! Broken my good new skipping rope... Matt, Matt, the great big sap—that's what you are, a great big sap!"

With a roar he was up, he caught her arm. She let go of the skipping rope and ran as fast as she could against that wall of air pushing against her chest, as fast as it would let her go. Yet her legs seemed weak, waving in mid-air but never moving; just peddling away in mid-air.

Somehow she reached the back gate, opened it. Matt was panting beside her. He picked up the garbage can lid and lifted it high and threatening. She yelled, and just as she got the gate open he banged the lid down WHAM, on the top of her head.

She screamed again, breaking away and stumbling towards the kitchen steps. The door opened; Dora came out and picked her up.

Matt still stood at the gate, the garbage can lid dangling from his raised arm.

"Get out! Get out, you wicked boy!" screamed Dora. Then she took Elizabeth inside and reported the story to mother.

After that, Matt stopped going to kindergarten. He was locked up in his own yard, behind a fence. She never had to hold his hand again.

The Two Willies

In those days, before anyone dreamed of dressing children to look like grown-ups; when "tussore" silk frocks were embroidered with cross-stitch and when black cotton stockings, ribbed, and high button boots, cork-screw curls and butterfly hair ribbons were regulation apparel for the small girl—in those days Elizabeth had no second-hand knowledge of the feeling of love. The strange sensation that choked her heart was closer to pain than to joy. The more she hugged it into herself the more did she want to burst into a hundred pieces. Yet she knew it had to be a secret, shared with no one. A mingling of sweetness and longing; and a name, humming through her head. The name, Willie.

Actually there were two Willies, living on the same block in West Winnipeg; and each one had a part in awaking her feelings. Across the street from her house was Wee Willie, the little two-year-old she looked after on those long afternoons when "the doctor said" she could not join the other children at school. And then, right next door to her, was Big Willie—Willie Hall, the high school boy. He it was who in summer-time took her for rides on his handle bars and in winter let her come and help him shovel snow off the sidewalk; her tiny shovel rasping against the ice, her small voice plying him with questions. He always listened seriously, and answered seriously . . . not like so many grown-ups. Perhaps he was lonely too, living with that very cross church-going mother. Anyway it seemed to happen every spring, when she heard the rushing sound of snow melting, of water gurgling and singing underneath the icy crust; when the first crows whooped and swooped in a black stagger against the dazzling blue; she would feel this strange excitement running up and down her left side; and she would sit and wait for the moment when Willie came riding home from school with his "Hello, Elizabeth!" He always gave her a special, lighted up smile; his short blonde hair was bushy like a wheatfield.

With Wee Willie the feeling was strong also; but different. Not a hurt, but a tender feeling such as you had when bending over a flower bed. At first he had been just a baby in a carriage, wheeled up and down the wooden sidewalk by Mrs. Weeks, his mother. Then he had become the baby whom Elizabeth was allowed to push. Last, he was a toddler Elizabeth called for, every afternoon at two, to take out for a walk. If he was awake, that is. If he wasn't awake Elizabeth sat on Mrs. Weeks' front steps and waited. Finally the door would open, and there would be Willie in a clean white piqué romper, held under his mother's arm, kicking away to show that he wanted to walk with Elizabeth.

"Your baby's ready!" young Mrs. Weeks would smile; and from her starched neat apron pocket she pulled out a nickel. "For an ice cream cone!"

"Oh, thank you!" Elizabeth wasn't supposed to take money from the neighbours, but Mrs. Weeks always looked so hurt if she didn't. Anyway she wouldn't buy a cone with it; she'd put it in her piggy bank, just before supper.

Now she had the street and Willie all to herself, for the other children were at school. Sometimes she pulled him around in a go-cart, up and down, up and down; but as his legs grew stronger he was able to walk beside her, take her hand and follow her across the street to her own yard. He was a roly-poly baby, very solemn, with fair hair she brushed back with her doll brush. She treated him rather like a doll, undoing his red leggings when the whim seized her, then carefully buttoning them up again; lifting him up suddenly into the doll buggy before he knew what was happening. Wee Willie did not mind.

One day in early June when the baby robins were falling out of their nests, learning to fly, Elizabeth felt it was time that Willie Weeks should learn to climb. Climbing was something she enjoyed supremely, herself; it would be fun for Willie to learn and to follow her when she climbed the high back fence surrounding the vegetable garden. At the point where this fence turned a sharp corner and bumped into the wall of the house, father had his cucumber frame. Elizabeth's game was to go into the back garden, climb up the cucumber frame and from there to the top of the high board fence. She could always come down by putting a foot on the lower, more secure fence that ran around to the front. She decided that this time Wee Willie could do it too.

With much grunting and heaving Willie was persuaded to climb along the cucumber frame, not putting his foot into the glass; and then stand ready beside the fence, his head scarcely showing over the top of it. Elizabeth climbed up ahead of him, then turned back, leaning along the ledge on her stomach. She held out her arms to Willie.

"Come, Willie. Come on up. Jump!" His pudgy hands met hers, trustingly; and Elizabeth half hauled, half scraped him onto the top of the high fence. "There, isn't that fun, Wee Willie? See, there's the whole world down below." Willie surveyed the situation, his round eyes wide as moons.

"Down dere?" he pointed.

"Yes, we'll get down there, dearie. Just wait till your Elizabeth gets her breath."

He sat contentedly, swinging his legs as she did and watching the cars and wagons going along past the firehall. Suddenly the firehall bell clanged!

"Now you're going to see something, Willie. Watch!"

From their high vantage point they could see, kitty-corner, the great red doors of the firehall burst open, the terrible clatter of hooves on the pavement as the huge grey horses pounded out in pairs, shaking their manes. Behind them were attached the firewagons, the thick hose wound around them, and the firemen clambering on, jamming on their sou'westers as the wagon thundered out onto the square. They swung around the corner and right past Elizabeth and Willie, up Centre Street.

"Fi—ah! Fia—ah!" Wee Willie bounced with excitement: his short legs beat against the boards, his body tipped backwards, then forwards. He was falling! Elizabeth grabbed hold of his red playsuit just as he slipped down the side of the fence. Then the weight of him pulled her over and she tumbled to the ground, plump on her knees.

"O-o-h, Willie!" she gasped, looking up. For there was Willie, hanging half way down, the back of his suit caught on a nail. He hung there like a sack, his legs and arms waving.

"O-o-h, Willie!" She didn't stop to think how lucky it was he hadn't fallen full force on the pavement. Instead she wrung her hands trying to think how she would get him off the nail. Pushing and heaving upwards did no good.

"Willie, jump! Jump! can't you?" But all Willie could do was to swing from side to side, wildly kicking with his legs and thrashing with his hands. Elizabeth didn't dare run for help, for fear the grown-ups wouldn't let her take Willie out again. She just had to get him down; she just had to.

Finally she got a wooden box, stood on it, and from there she lifted, heaved and pushed until Willie's leggings at last came free. She jerked him forward into her arms and then collapsed on the ground beside him. Willie was so surprised he didn't even cry.

"But your leggings, Willie—O—oh look! They're all torn." Willie couldn't look, he seemed glad to be on the ground again, free to run ahead and make Elizabeth catch him. She ran and seized his hand.

"We'll have to go to Mummie, Willie."

"Mu-u-um," said Willie.

"Yes. Home to Mummie." At the thought, she could feel her heart miss a thump. Whatever would Mrs. Weeks say? That tear in his pants! For Elizabeth would have to show it to her—she'd just have to. And then what would Mrs. Weeks ask? *How* did it tear?

Feeling hot and sweaty Elizabeth marched Willie slowly across the street and up the steps, rang his doorbell. Mrs. Weeks opened the door quite quickly, as if she had been standing there all the time.

"I think Willie'd better come in now," Elizabeth explained, gulping. "You see, he tore his pants."

Mrs. Weeks looked. Fear alone kept Elizabeth standing there unable to move. Mrs. Weeks threw Willie up in her arms. "Oh, that little rip!" she said, "That's nothing. I can mend it in no time."

Elizabeth took a deep breath. She turned to go, but Mrs. Weeks called her back. "Just a minute, dear—you forgot your pay." And she pressed a nickel into Elizabeth's hand. "For being such a good babysitter," Mrs. Weeks smiled.

Elizabeth flushed scarlet. "Oh, I couldn't. I couldn't take it thank you. Mother says—"

"It'll be all right. I'll tell your mother. Take it now, and run along. . . See you tomorrow?"

Elizabeth ducked her head in reply, rushed down the steps clutching the ill-gotten gains. This money she wouldn't spend at all, she would put it safely in her piggy bank and help it to grow to five dollars! She ran home, climbed on a chair to the shelf in the dining-room where her little black pot stood, and stuffed the nickel in.

In the summer holidays she didn't see Willie Weeks, because she was away at the Lake of the Woods. And on her return it was a shock, like a slap in the face, to learn that Willie Weeks would soon be moving away, "going west". When she saw Elizabeth's face Mrs. Weeks dived into her purse and brought forth a silver ten-cent piece. "That's because you've been such a help to me," she said. Elizabeth glowed. She took the money without hesitating this time and went straight to her piggy bank.

The round metal box fell easily into her hand and then fell to the floor without a clank. It was empty! "Oh, Mummie, look, my bank's empty! And it's broken, it won't open!" Mother pressed the lid, and it rolled off into her hand. There wasn't a penny in the bank.

"But I had nearly five dollars! See, it is marked on the marker, four dollars and thirty-nine cents!" She let out a wail.

"Hush. Hush child. Yes, it looks as though someone had been pilfering... I wonder if anything else has been touched?" And mother told her to run along, Daddy would give her the money back. Then mother went to the telephone.

Elizabeth had forgotten all about it when, a week later, father called her to come and look at her piggy bank. "Lift it." She did so, and felt the money heavy inside. "Oh, goody, goody! How did you find the money, Daddy?"

"Oh, we found it."

That was all she could get out of him. Later mother told her that during the holidays a gang of boys, led by someone who knew the house, had got in by the cellar window and stolen the money so they could all go to a moving picture.

"The boys on this street?" She was horrified.

"Yes."

"But Mummie, that's *stealing*!"

"I know. The boy who did it is very sorry and he won't do it again."

"Was it Gordie?"

"No."

"Was it Charlie?"

"No."

"I know who—it was Matt!"

"Oh no, dear, a bigger boy. Now don't you ask any more questions because I am not going to tell you. Daddy has had a talk with the boy and he was very sorry; it has taught him a lesson, I dare say."

Every night, for a time, Elizabeth lay in bed puzzling over all the boys she had fought and argued with on the street; all the boys who hated father because he made them keep off the boulevard grass. Especially there was Everett, the boy father had taken across his knees and spanked, because he was swinging on father's nursling oak tree.

"I bet it was Everett," she thought.

Then, long afterward, at Christmas time, there was a ring at the doorbell. A boy wanted to see Elizabeth. "Oh, hello," she said; there stood
Willie Hall. In his arms he held a large cradle, carved in oak. "For your
dolly," he said. "I made it at manual."

A cradle! A real doll's cradle that rocked! She was enchanted. "Oh,
thank you, thank you, Willie. Daddy-y!" she called. "Come and see what
Willie made for me."

"Isn't that fine! That's very well built, Willie. Real style to that." And
father rocked it with his foot. Then he held out a gift to Willie—a flash
light!

"Oh, thank you, sir." Willie's face turned red. And when he took the
present he shook father's hand till Elizabeth thought it would be crushed.
Almost she thought there were tears in his eyes. "Thank you," said Willie again, as he rushed out the door into the snow.

That evening, putting her dolly to bed in the cradle, pretending it was
Wee Willie who lay there, being rocked to sleep—Elizabeth felt a sharp
and sickening pain in the old place, around her heart. And suddenly Elizabeth knew: it was Willie Hall, Big Willie, who had stolen her piggy
bank! . . . She lay awake for a long time that night, staring into the dark.

Mrs. Spy

War broke out before she was five. So war was a part of childhood, a wave on the beach indistinguishable from others except that it carried some additional excitement. There were bands to follow, as they paraded up and down the wide prairie streets; colourful hussars with nodding plumes, the shrill insistence of the bugle, the command of the drum. There were newsboys to imitate, as they rushed into the street waving headlines: "Ex-tra-a! Ex-tra-a!" Elizabeth collected newspapers from under the playroom couch; she too walked up and down the block shouting: "Ex-tra!" But nobody bought a paper from her. Mrs. Hall and Mrs. Hendry sat on their verandahs, rocking away, and just smiling as Elizabeth offered her wares.

"Are the Germans winning?" Mrs. Hendry asked.

"No, the Canadians are!" she answered, blithely. And moved on up the street.

Those Germans! Up the street, right here at home, Germans were living. Spies! Of course, nobody knew *for sure* that the couple living in the house beside the field were spies: but everybody knew they were Germans, who couldn't talk English well. They had moved in only the year before the war started. The children had often passed by that little brown house on their way to play in the field: but now they rarely did so. Still, it was a good place to play; and when Peggy suggested one morning that they play war and dig trenches and shoot at each other, like the boys did, Elizabeth had a sudden longing to get back to that dear field, empty, but full of clover and hay and grasshoppers.

They set out early, cautiously. And before long they were blissfully unaware of any movement on the street or any life other than their own game. As the sun moved higher in the sky they grew hot and thirsty; but they played on. Suddenly Elizabeth, as she ran along a ditch below the sidewalk, came upon a pipe and a real water tap.

"Oo-h!" she cried, "Come and help me turn it, Peggy!" They struggled, four small hands on the tap; and then it gave, spurting cool water over their arms. "Goody. Now we can have a drink!"

Elizabeth stooped first, because she was the finder: she put her mouth under the tap: choked and spluttered. Then it was Peggy's turn.

From far away a voice shook them: "Hey! Don' do dat!" They whirled around, to face the house alongside the field—the little brown house. On the front porch stood the spy's wife, fat, round-cheeked and talking to them fast, in a thick accent.

"Dat water no good," said Mrs. Spy. "All dirty. Don't you trink. Kom over here. Kom!" She beckoned with her arm.

As though mesmerized, they moved forward. "Come, come" signalled the arm of Mrs. Spy. They found themselves moving through her gate, up the walk to the front steps.

"You tirsty?" Her round face beamed. "I give you to trink. Kom here, along the side, to the back. In the kitchen I give you to trink, heh?"

They did not dare look at each other; but holding hands tight they did exactly as she told them; along the narrow walk, and around to the back stoop. "Won't you kom in?" Mrs. Spy asked. They shook their heads. This was definitely as far as she would get them.

"Vel then, I bring a cup." And she went inside.

"I bet she'll give us poison," Elizabeth muttered, darkly.

"You can drink it then—I won't!" said Peggy.

"S-hh. Just wait and see."

"Here you are, *kinder*!" Mrs. Spy had reappeared, with a large white cup with pink roses painted on the side.

"I don't want any, thank you," said Peggy.

"Vel then—you—you are the tirsty one!" Mrs. Spy beamed at Elizabeth.

Elizabeth took the cup. Then she turned round slowly, looking down the alley as she lifted it to her lips. Peggy was watching her, fascinated.

"Gee, Peggy, it must be nearly lunchtime," she said loudly. "When I've drunk this we'd better get home."

Peggy nodded. While Elizabeth talked she pretended to sip the water, her back to the stoop. Then, when Mrs. Spy seemed busy for a moment, picking up the milk bottle with a clatter, Elizabeth bent down gently and let the water pour from the cup to the ground.

"There!" she said, turning round fast. She ran to the back steps and offered up the empty cup. "Thank you very much."

"It's goot, eh? You come again here for water when you play, eh?"

"Yes, we will, thank you," the little girls chorused. Then they ran back down the alley as fast as they could. They never stopped running till they got home.

"I bet it was poisoned," gasped Peggy. "That was smart, you acted smart, Elizabeth, throwing it away."

Elizabeth nodded, too breathless to reply. She felt like saying a prayer, then and there, of thanks to God for saving her from the Germans.

The Guardian Angel

Elizabeth never protested when it was suggested that she spend a day or two at Granny's house. Although she was familiar with her father's house and the people in it, she never felt so completely comfortable there as at Granny's house, with Aunt Maudie to talk to. It was as if her own place was made of boards and railings and shingles and paint, with a very special fence around it to keep out the baying dogs and boys; while her Granny's place was a nest, lined with comfort, tended by loving hands.

Not that there was any luxury about Granny's house. Far from it. The neighbourhood, if anything, was tough; the neighbours were poor and hard-working; her two uncles rented empty lots in summer to grow the winter's supply of potatoes, corn, tomatoes and green beans. Aunt Maudie "did up" the vegetables for the winter; or things like beans she would salt down in a crock. She was always making jams and jellies, and the bittersweet smell of her *piccalilli* pervaded the house throughout September.

Unlike Elizabeth's mother, Aunt Maudie loved to cook. She seemed always to have a spoon in her hand, beating up this, or tasting that—her prematurely white hair standing on end from the heat of the stove. She loved to show Elizabeth how: the proper way of beating up a cake, or of making brown sugar sauce for the spice pudding. Noontime was dinner-time, when Uncle got home from work; there would be a savoury stew with dumplings; or steak and mashed potatoes; or ham with stewed tomatoes, sprinkled with soda crackers. After the pudding there would be a lump of maple sugar to suck. For Granny had followed her grown-up children west from the Eastern Townships—that golden country Aunt Maudie talked about, where arbutus hid in the spring woods and boys and men came with pails to the maple grove, for the sugaring off. Yes, there just had to be maple syrup in Granny's pantry.

That pantry! It was almost like a laboratory, with so many experiments going on that they had overflowed from the cupboards and onto the long sideboard opposite the sink. A dab of jam, a jelly put to set, a sample of pickle, a bowl of milk souring to make cottage cheese, some garden cress sprouting from a jug, enough butter for one piece of toast. Aunt Maudie loved to cook and to make doll's clothes, but she seemed to revel in disorder too. It would have been a bad day at Granny's house if anyone like Doris had been sent to clean up.

Somehow, Elizabeth did not mind the clutter. Every object left lying around—a lacquer tray with pins and needles in it; a vase stuffed with string; the little wooden box made like a trunk, with a tiny key, full of old stamps and a lock of hair: each thing took on meaning from the warmth of the kitchen range, the dazzle of green leaf and red geranium in the dining-room window, the high trill of Granny's canary, always singing; Granny's own chuckle and Aunt Maudie's patient voice always explaining, always interested in what the child was doing. "Look," she would say, and show a pattern in a knitting book. "You could make that doll's sweater, Elizabeth, now you've made a start with your knitting. No, hold the needle this way, dear." And somehow, one came to believe, however awkward one was with hands, that it would be possible to knit a sweater; or, as might be, to make a cake.

Only in the evening, after supper, did Granny's house seem a bit unfamiliar, awesome. It was so quiet! The green glass shade of the lamp would be lowered by a pulley arrangement to the exact centre of the dining-room table. Aunt Maudie would pull out all her coloured silks and begin making French knots on a doily, while Granny took out the long pen with an imitation quill on the end, to write her weekly letter to Uncle, away at the war.

Elizabeth sat with a book. Behind her the bird had been put to bed, his cage wrapped in a shawl; the only sound would come from the pendulum clock, tick tock, tick tock. There was no Susie to romp with. It was quiet, quiet.

Suddenly the clock would strike its resonant, throaty notes, and she would count with it to eight o'clock. "Bedtime," Aunt Maudie would say: and she would smile gently, laying down her doily, and blink at Elizabeth, her pale blue eyes flickering behind gold-rimmed spectacles. Her face was sweet to look at, sweet and patient; and her fine wispy hair, much whiter than Granny's, seemed to shine like a white light around her face.

Alone in the bedroom, Granny's bedroom, smelling of camphorated oil, squills and friar's balsam, she felt strange again; and not as safe, even, as in the small world of the dining-room. But she undressed and climbed into Granny's great bed, with the shining brass foot-rail and round brass knobs. Aunt Maudie kissed her goodnight and then Granny, small and hunched and in her serious mood, came upstairs to hear prayers.

"And God bless Mummy and Daddy and Sister and kill all the bad Germans and help us win the war!"

"Why, Elizabeth!" Granny exclaimed. "Who taught you to say a prayer like that?"

"I just say it."

"Does your mother hear you saying it?"

"She said to say it. Don't you want it, Granny—don't you want the war to end and Uncle to come home?"

"Of course I do... But perhaps there is a little German girl named Elizabeth, who wants her Uncle to come home, too."

"O-o-h," This was a new idea, never mentioned on Elizabeth's street. "Well, don't let it worry you, dear. Off to dreams, sweet dreams."

At home, Granny knew very well, Elizabeth could never get to sleep quickly. There were too many stories in her head, humming and humming; and that witch under the bed. Mother was always telling Granny how bad Elizabeth was about going to sleep, how she would call and call and mother would have to come upstairs again to rub her legs, "all stretchy". This she did even though father was saying to her irritably at the foot of the stairs, "Leave the child alone, she'll drop off." But eventually it was father who gave in, too; for if Elizabeth kept on lying awake, tight as a bow, she knew he would come up and rub the back of her neck gently, gently. Then she would fall asleep.

Granny replied that all this was nonsense, and no child would call *her* upstairs again. So Elizabeth knew there was no help in Granny's house. It was all so quiet, no talk, no piano playing, that she could almost hear, downstairs in Granny's house, that dining-room clock going tick tock, tick tock. She was asleep.

One night at Granny's she awakened, screaming. There had been a terrible dream, a long grey corridor underground, with wooden boards as on a ship, slanting downwards, downwards, and a donkey chasing her with loud clomping hooves, chasing and chasing her down endless corridors, cold in the underground. She tore herself up from it, sweating, her heart pounding. And there, lighting all the darkness, at the foot of the brass railing of Granny's bed—there stood a golden angel, with wings high as the ceiling. The angel was smiling—her guardian angel. No word was said, but the hush of his wings filled the room with peace. She sank back to the pillow, quiet.

"Elizabeth!" It was Aunt Maudie, come into the room, standing by the side of the bed. "What is it, dear?"

"S-sh. Look there, Aunt Maudie—Look!" But as they looked, the vision was gone.

"I had a bad dream," she murmured. "I saw an angel." And she fell asleep again; safe in Granny's house.

The Sparrows

It was so hot that summer day that Elizabeth and her friend Peggy sought out the coolest corner of the yard. This was on the north side, a narrow overgrown patch between the house and Mrs. Hall's fence. Too damp and shady a place it was for father to have bothered with, as garden, so grass grew as it willed, long-stemmed and refreshing to the face.

They lay dreamily on their stomachs, side by side, chewing grass roots and looking through the oblong bars of wire fence into the emerald world of Mrs. Hall's neatly clipped lawn. Here it seemed as if all the sparrows in the street had foregathered, hopping about in search of grubs.

"They can't catch worms like robins do," Elizabeth observed.

"What are they eating anyway? Nothing but dirt."

"Maybe they chew grass like dogs. It's medicine for dogs, you know."

"Cats like catnip."

"Well, look at all the catnip here, and our cat never comes to eat it."

"Maybe you have to show her."

Conversation lagged as Elizabeth considered the possibilities of this idea. But neither of them really wanted to stir. It was fun to be lying here so secretly, with no one knowing where you were. Just the two of them, shut away even from the blink of the sun. Nobody could guess you were there. Unless you counted God. He was always about, they told you in Sunday School, always looking at whatever you did. You'd think he'd get tired sometimes, just watching all the dull things grown-ups bother with. Always doing good, or visiting the sick, like Mrs. Hall, because she was a Pillar of the Church, so father said.

Just as Elizabeth was thinking about her, Mrs. Hall's front door opened sharply. She must be going down-town, for she turned to make sure that the door was locked. Then she marched down the steps as square and solid as a pillar, but with the added glory of a mauve muslin dress draped around herself. Mrs. Hall paused for a moment at the gate, cast a benign look around her trim garden, and then sallied out into the burning street. She hadn't even seen them! The two little girls giggled, happy because they would not have to speak politely to Mrs. Hall. She was the head of the Sunday School and one could not be too careful. Elizabeth began to think about God again, and the sparrows.

"D'you think God just lets them be hungry like that?"

"God sees the little sparrow fall," Peggy began, and Elizabeth took it up, humming the refrain: "He loves me too, He loves me too, I know He loves me too-oo." She shifted sideways, leaning on her elbow as she eyed the sparrows, critically.

"I guess God really put *us* here so we could look after *them*," she suggested.

"You mean *us*—here, now?"

"Uh, huh. Anybody who sees birds hungry like that."

"Has your Mum got any breadcrumbs, Elizabeth?"

"There's always some in the breadbox."

"Well, let's go get 'em then. That would be a good deed."

Elizabeth's eyes lit up. Weren't they always telling you in Sunday School to do a good deed? Not just on Sundays, but on weekdays? She jumped to her feet, pulling Peggy with her. "Come *on*!" she cried.

There was no one in the kitchen, but they crept about stealthily on their toes. "Here's the bread box," Elizabeth whispered. "S-sh," she admonished, as Peggy could not help chuckling. Both heads peered into it, bumping each other. "Ouch!" cried Peggy. She giggled again.

"S-sh!" Elizabeth pulled out a crusty white loaf, Daddy's favourite kind. Her hand clawed the bottom of the tin and came out with a haul of old crusts. "There don't seem to be any crumbs," she reported.

"Well, won't these do?" Peggy took a crust in her hand, began to nibble at it. "Tastes all right," she said, "but it's awful hard."

"The bird beaks might break on it." Elizabeth looked doubtful.

"Can't we crack it up?" They tried, but their small fingers only managed to get scratched. A few smaller pieces yielded to their pressure.

"I know what!" said Elizabeth. "We'll make them soft—wet them under the tap. That's what Doris does when she's making bread dressing."

They found a bagful of dried bread and soaked it properly by wetting it in a basin. Carefully Elizabeth led the way out of the kitchen door and around the house to the cool shade. They set the basin on Mrs. Hall's fence and clambered over it themselves. Promptly all the sparrows shut up shop and flew away.

"Oh dear," said Peggy.

"Never mind, they'll come back," Elizabeth assured her. "Just wait till they see all this white bread."

With abandon they dipped their hands into the basin and cast their bread upon the grasses, right and left. Elizabeth remembered a picture she had seen in "Bible Stories", of a sower going forth to sow, scattering the seed with a fine gesture. She felt the same way herself, marching up and down the carpet of lawn. But all too soon the basin was empty.

They stood there, looking up into the maple trees to see where the sparrows could be. "Come back to our place," Elizabeth whispered. "If we lie quiet in the grass where we were before, then we can watch them feasting."

"Poor little things," Peggy said. "They must be just starving."

Back in their lair the children lay down again, watching and waiting.

Elizabeth began pulling up long grasses and plaiting them into a crown. These she put in Peggy's hair, but Peggy did not like the feel of them. "Don't," she said, and threw the wreath away.

"Stop. You'll frighten the birds."

"But they haven't come yet!" Peggy was pouting.

"You have to be patient, that's what bird-watchers are, mother read it in a book."

"We're not watchers, we're feeders. Like at my uncle's farm, when you throw grain to the chickens they run so fast—they gobble it all up quick."

"Oh, I bet they're *tame* chickens," Elizabeth countered quickly. Our sparrows are *wild* . . . Look, there's one now, see him?"

"Where?"

"Over there, by Mrs. Hall's steps." Yes, there was one bold adventurer, but he was busy in the gravel walk. He did not even glance towards the green grass, now white with manna.

"Aw, let's not wait here any more," said Peggy. Let's get your ball and play alairy."

"All right." Elizabeth rose reluctantly. She hopped about on one leg for a moment, for the other was all tingly, from lying in one spot so long. "I guess maybe if we go right away the sparrows will come back. They're smart, you know. They know we're *people*."

"I thought we were s'posed to be God," Peggy replied, sourly.

They moved quickly to the other side of the house, where the sunlight suddenly felt inviting, a warm touch on the arm. A tiny breeze had arisen and this stirred them into activity; they hopped about first on one foot, then on the other, playing ball like small birds bouncing after crumbs.

Much later in the afternoon Peggy was called home.

"Gee, I forgot, my cousin is coming for supper. Mum said I had to get home early and get cleaned up."

"G'bye."

"G'bye." Elizabeth sat down desultorily on the front steps. A book she had been looking at in the morning lay there open, pages fluttering gently in the wind. She picked it up, and began to work out the words. Hazily, beyond her in the street, she heard the sound of footsteps clattering up and down the board walk; the clop clop, cloppity clop of a delivery horse; the far-away cries of other children. Then, crossing the hard paved corner in front of her house, high heels sounded. She looked up. It was Mrs. Hall, returning from her shopping.

"Hello, Mrs. Hall," she called out.

"Why, hello, Elizabeth." Mrs. Hall crossed the boulevard, stood for a moment leaning over Elizabeth's gate. "How are you this afternoon?"

"Just fine." Elizabeth smiled, hugging her knees. She watched Mrs. Hall move along the sidewalk to her own gate, open it, and walk towards the steps.

"What in the—"

Elizabeth stood up, her hand tightening on her book. "What's the matter?"

"Did *you* do this?" Mrs. Hall's voice was no longer smiling and pleasant.

"Why—er—Peggy and I—" Her lips began to get dry. "We saw the birds on your lawn, Mrs. Hall. They looked so hungry, we thought—"

"Hungry! Indeed. Why didn't you carry out your charitable impulses on your father's lawn, then? I imagine he would have plenty to say. Why, it's disgraceful. Just come over here and look at the mess."

Elizabeth went, her legs weighted. She looked. She saw, as if through Mrs. Hall's eyes, the smooth green lawn dotted with sloppy bits of white, straggling crusts of bread strewn all over the lawn, like a patchwork quilt.

Elizabeth blushed. "I-I guess they didn't eat it all up," she said, lamely.

"I guess they didn't. But I guess someone else will have to eat it up— clear it up, anyway. Have you got a basin?"

"Oh, yes!" Elizabeth bolted up the steps and into the house. She felt all choked up inside, but she couldn't cry. "Oh, the poor birds, the poor little birds," she was saying to herself. And underneath: "That mean old woman, wait'll I tell Peggy what a mean thing that Mrs. Hall is."

When she got outside again, and over on Mrs. Hall's side of the fence she realized, emphatically, that there was no way of telling Peggy. Not just now. Worse, there was no way of calling Peggy to help. Yet Peggy had done it, just as much as she had. It was Peggy's idea! And now she had to go and clean it up, all alone.

"Ugh!" She stopped and picked up one soggy crust of bread. It felt "gooey", like a white worm. Mrs. Hall stood there by the steps, watching, so Elizabeth had to stoop down again and again, and pick up another piece. Each time she touched the cold sliminess she recoiled. Each time she felt Mrs. Hall's eyes gluing her to the grass; so she went on, and on. Her back ached. Her fingers were damp and clammy from handling the soggy stuff. But somehow, to the uttermost parts of the lawn she travailed, until every piece was finally garnered in. The basin was full—heavy and soggy and full.

Elizabeth picked it up in her arms and moved forward, dizzily. Mrs. Hall had gone inside without even thanking her. The sparrows hadn't thanked her, either. As for God, what had He been doing all this time?

"He loves me too, He loves me too—" Silly old hymn. Why did she have to think of that tune now?

She marched to the gate, stopped, and kicked Mrs. Hall's velvet lawn one savage kick. Then she ran.

Christmas

Elizabeth awakened early, feeling that the black night had verged into grey, somewhere beyond the winter blind. At first she lay still, intent on remembering the feeling of the night before, Christmas Eve, when she lay curled in this same bed, wondering at what moment the bells would jingle, the roof would shake. Would Santa *really* climb down the chimney, read her note, and then tiptoe up to her room? Those bells jingling—surely she had heard them, in the night? Bells, or the echo of bells? And had it happened?

Her eyes opened, shifted to the head of the bed, and craned upward. There it was, the red wool stocking hanging just as she had left it, from the white bedpost. But it was bulgy and bursting, and leering from the top was a clown's head! She laughed, and reached up, chuckling, her hands fumbling with the excitement. She was not allowed to see her big presents till the Tree was unveiled, but her stocking was her very own private joy. So it was true, Santa had come!

Nuts, tangerine oranges, cluster raisins—all the treats of Christmas—

and a sachet, a hankie, a tiny celluloid doll, just right for the doll's house. She dreamed an hour away, tingling with the newness, the differentness. Having new things, however small, made oneself feel new again. The old Elizabeth had fallen asleep on Christmas Eve and a new one arose clothed in golden garments, bursting with song.

On the stairs, after breakfast, she practised flying. Only once had she succeeded in really and truly flying, a mad swift flight down the cellar steps. "Mummy! Mummy!" She had come running into the dining-room where mother was immersed in pen and ink and pale green sheets of typing paper brought from father's office. "Mummy, come and see! I can fly!"

"Fly?" Her mother, as if in a trance, had yielded to the tugging hand and had followed through the kitchen to the top of the cellar steps.

"What are you going to do, Elizabeth?"

"Why, show you how I can fly. All the way down the steps!"

"Oh, it's a pretend game, is it?"

"No, a true one. Because I did it Mummy, I did it!"

"Show me."

"Well—I—" She stood at the top, ready to take off. Then a strange fear gripped her. She had forgotten how! Yet she knew, she knew! She gave herself a little push, a jump forward—and fell on the second step.

"Why, Elizabeth, silly child, you can't jump all that way down!"

"But I did, honestly, Mum. And I wasn't jumping. I was flying!"

"Well, be careful, dear. I wouldn't try it there. You'll land on the hard cement floor."

She had moved upstairs again, bewildered. For she *had* flown. But mother suggested she put in her flying hours on the front hall stairs, heavily carpeted as they were with a thick green rug, and padded underneath with soft pads, and buckled down at the corners with brass buckles. So here she was again, on Christmas morning, such a glorious morning she felt she could do anything, anything: certainly she could fly again! Up on the landing she stood, trying and trying to let go. But it was all spoiled, somehow. She had forgotten how to fly.

Instead, she slid down the bannister; then sat on the stairs pretending she was baby Jesus singing "Carol, swee-e-tly carol." Then her own carols, sung as the wind blows... She was an angel on the golden stairway, singing her way up to heaven!

She was interrupted by mother's voice: "Elizabeth! Time to get ready for church."

"Yes, Mummy." Today she made no fuss about it. On most Sundays, when she had to go to church with mother, she protested all the way, thinking of the trouble she would have trying to sit still. In the pew, after praying, mother would give her a long black steel hairpin and she would take out her handkerchief and make a hairpin doll, whose adventures developed beneath the drone of the sermon. But at Christmas time, church was different.

This day the church was crowded with people all standing up and shouting carols till the roof seemed to quake. It was easy to see the shepherds watching their flocks and the crowds of angels sitting on a cloud and shouting "Noel". She didn't know all the words of the hymns, but she could sing the refrains, over and over, her face lifted, it seemed, far above the press of people.

When they came out of the glowing light of the church, gentle with greetings and warm with music, the new snow would be spread softly along the boulevard, sparkling like glass; in other places dove blue like the undersides of angels' wings. She would run and slide, run and slide, all the way home. Then, in front of the house, there would be Susan, playing with her last year's sleigh.

When mother called them indoors, great whiffs of turkey came from the kitchen; and there they found father, wrapped all around in a hoover apron, punching a fork into the great bird and declaring that all was ready. It did not always happen that father cooked the Christmas dinner, but this year Doris was away in the country. Mother couldn't cook, but father loved it. So long, that is, as he only had to do it about once a year.

But the big time of day, for Elizabeth and Susan, came in the afternoon, when the rolling doors of the drawing-room were pushed open and a troop of children poured in, breathless with excitement. The Tree stood in a corner, from floor to ceiling loaded with parcels, coloured globes, festoons and tinsel. And there beside it was a sleigh—two sleighs— one for Elizabeth, one for Susan: "With Love from Santa!" They clapped their hands, not daring yet to touch their presents until everyone was seated in a circle.

This was father's great moment. He sat beside the tree, chuckling with anticipation, while Elizabeth, dressed in cotton batten, became the Snow Fairy who would distribute the gifts. There was a present for everyone in the room, father had seen to that. He had wrapped something up for every child on the street. Elizabeth laughed with the wonder of it as she gave out the gifts and heard the children saying: "Oh-h, thank you, Big Bear" to father. Father loved it. Like a king he was in his own hand-made kingdom, with Elizabeth his handmaiden.

Yet it had to finish; it had to end. There would be a mountain of coloured tissue paper on the floor and Elizabeth would dive into it, looking for that new book. Father would fall asleep on the sofa, his hands folded and fingers crossed. Mother would sit reading and Susan would clamour to go outside. "Sleigh out, Lizbeth. Sleigh out."

Reluctantly she left the warmth, the room still shimmering with silver and red, silver and green. In the hall she struggled with over-stockings and moccasins, the heavy coat, the red toque. "Do I have to wear a veil, Mama?"

"No, I don't think it's as cold as that out today. But don't stay out long."

Elizabeth's new sleigh was dark green, with a red rose painted in the middle. Susan had a red sleigh, not so big. They moved out into the late prairie afternoon where the cold sun laid only the lightest of its long fingers over the snow, pointing down hill. For there was a slight rise they called "the hill" and here they came, to lie on their tummies, guiding the sleigh with one foot down and down to where dozens of children tumbled.

"Hi, Liz."

"Hi. I got a new sleigh."

"Oh-h. Isn't it pretty!"

Boys as well as girls crowded round the special sleigh.

"Who give it ya?" a big boy asked.

"Why, Santa Claus." Derisive hoots greeted this remark, she did not know why. She pulled the sleigh closer, sat on it.

"Don't you know who Santa really is?"

"Of course I do. He's a Saint."

More laughter greeted this remark. "You don't know much, Kid. Why, there ain't no Santa Claus—he's just your father and mother."

Her father and mother! All that Christmas joy, and it was just father and mother. "You're telling a lie," she shouted back. "I'll go and ask my Mum."

"Ask her then, ask her!" The boys taunted.

Elizabeth tugged at the rope of her sleigh, swung it around. "Come on, Susie," she said. Susan followed behind, obedient and solemn. Wherever Elizabeth went, Susan had to go.

Elizabeth walked slowly but steadily up the rise and across the firehall corner. Outside her own gate she abandoned the new sleigh and ran fast into the house. Mother was still reading a book in the drawing-room.

"Mother, Mother! Those mean boys were just lying, weren't they?"

"Why, whatever do you mean, dear? What happened?"

She answered in a shrill voice, begging for reassurance. "They said there was not really any Santa Claus—it was just you and Daddy gave us all the presents—" Her voice broke. "That's not true, is it, Mummy? Is it?"

Instead of taking her in her arms for a hug, mother let the book drop. "Well, Jeff?" she asked, turning to father. He had wakened up, though still lying on the sofa and rubbing his eyes. "What's this about? What's this?"

Elizabeth ran to him, knelt beside him. "There *is* a Santa Claus, isn't there, Daddy?"

"Well—there is; and again, there isn't, Elizabeth."

"You mean it really is a lie—Santa's just a lie?"

"Say rather, Santa is a fairy story, girlie. A story that someone made up, that could be true—the idea behind it, that is."

Perhaps he went on further, but she didn't follow. She had grasped the one overhanging thing: there *was* no Santa! Those boys had been right. Her parents had lied!

And if so, if so—she ran from the room, up the soft carpeted stairs where she had flown, where she had carolled all morning. Now she *knew* she would never fly again; and singing would never be the same. . . Choking, she ran into her own little white room, and flung herself down on the bed, her arms encircling her head, a shield from the world. Only her bed was kind.

Anna

The week mother brought Polish Anna home from the Employment Bureau was the week when school was out: the family would be going to the Lake of the Woods for the summer. Anna was to come along too and learn to cook the Canadian way, and keep the cottage clean and look after the children.

"I hope she'll settle down there," mother said. "She's so homesick now, in the city, what shall we do with her in the country?"

Anna was quite heavy—"plump," father called her—but she moved lightly. Her shining brown hair was wound in coils at the nape of her neck; her wide brown eyes were the saddest Elizabeth had ever seen. Anna was not like the other "mother's helps" that followed one another, every few months, into the house, and out again. She only knew a few words of English: when she understood what was wanted of her she would nod her head fast and say: "Ya, Ya." When she did not understand, she cried. But Anna seemed lonelier than most girls, unable to find friends; frightened, as if she had never come to this country of her own free will.

45

Her brothers had died fighting in the war; that was all the family knew about her.

On the train trip to Keewatin Elizabeth and little Susie sat in a double seat with mother and the luggage; Anna sat alone in a single seat behind them, looking out of the window at the endless poplar bush, and crying.

"Is she still homesick, mother?"

"I expect so, dear. Just leave her alone."

But Elizabeth could not help peering over the top of the seat, whenever they stopped at a station, and telling Anna the name of it. Anna nodded, mutely, blowing her nose. Finally Elizabeth opened a bag of peanuts mother had bought her, and slipped into Anna's seat. "Peanuts. Goo-ood," Elizabeth urged. "Have some?"

Puzzled, Anna picked out a nut; Elizabeth showed her how to crack it and find the sweet kernel inside. Then Elizabeth put it between Anna's lips and laughed at the doubtful expression on Anna's face. "Go on. Eat it. You'll like it!" So finally Anna began crunching away; she even smiled a little. Elizabeth felt moved to come closer to the long black serge skirt, the stiff cotton blouse, and to feel the flowing warmth of Anna's bosom. "I like you," she confided. And whether Anna understood or not, she stopped crying. Elizabeth fell asleep.

After that, Anna was like a mother to Elizabeth. In the cottage perched on a rock, darkened with pine trees and the dark brown water of the Lake below, the two would sit on the steps shelling peas together, with Elizabeth telling Anna the words for things: or they would set out behind the house with lard pails, looking for raspberries or blueberries; and alone on the rock, resting for a moment on deep moss and gazing into the burning sky, Anna would sing to Elizabeth a plaintive Polish folksong. But she remained without laughter—sad. And whenever she did something wrong with the cooking or the housework or failed to go for the milk at the right time, when mother scolded her sharply, then Anna would go to her cubicle-like room, and cry. And outside her door, listening, Elizabeth would cry, too, but in an inward way she had not known before, with dry eyes.

When father came down for the week-ends, he tried to cheer Anna up. In the afternoon he would untie the rowboat and call the children to come for a row: "And bring Anna too." And mother might protest, saying Anna had to get the dinner prepared; but he would say she needed time off and they would all three pile in. Anna was nervous in the boat, but they showed her how to set foot in the centre, and then sit at the stern, holding the rudder. And after a while she seemed to be enjoying herself, nodding "Ya, Ya" and gazing far off towards the shrouded evergreen islands.

"Let's go to the Indian camp," father said. "I want to take some pictures."

"All right. Goody!" They clapped their hands. "But I thought Indians never let you take pictures," Elizabeth said.

"Oh, well, you never can tell."

Father rowed round the first point, and then round the second, till they came to the bare rocky "Indian Point" hillside where the tents were pitched. But as soon as their boat touched shore the half-naked, tousled Indian children scampered away, like ants scuttling into cracks; a tall young man moved down to the beach; and in the nearest teepee an old woman squatted on her heels, working with birchbark.

"You wanta buy baskets?" The man eyed father, expressionless.

"Well, not today, thanks. I bought some here before, a couple of weeks ago. . . You remember me?" He smiled, nodding towards the fat old woman. The gaps between her teeth flashed. "Beautiful design on the baskets," father said. "Where do you get the porcupine quills?" And to show what he meant, he picked a few up in his hand, passed them to Anna to feel. Anna looked surprised, touched them with her fingers. She looked up at the Indian youth, so brown and silent, and then down at the quills.

"I hunt them in the winter-time," the young man said. And father got him to tell a little about that. The old woman said nothing; but she was listening, you could tell.

"And now—how about a picture—would you mind if I take the old lady's picture?" Father was unslinging his camera.

Immediately Elizabeth wanted to turn and run back to the boat. But she was rooted there. She felt the dark mask coming over the young Indian's face. And the old woman cackled, her braids tossing.

"Can I make a nice picture of you—eh, mother?" father repeated. She looked at her son: then, "No no, no no," she insisted: her face showed no feelings.

"Well—too bad. Perhaps another time, eh? Such a picturesque place you have." Father spread out his hands, indicated the community of tee-pees, the white birch trees etched against evergreen and rock. "Too bad. Come along then, children."

They ran down to the rowboat, as if released from a spring. Only Anna moved leisurely: paused at the beach to turn and look at the Indian. He remained motionless, defensive; and he did not answer when father called "Goodbye" and pushed off from the shore.

"You shouldn't have gone there, Daddy," Elizabeth told him.

"Oh, what nonsense! It's nice to be friendly. . . If I'd bought a basket you'd see them soften up!"

"Why didn't the old lady ever stand up?" Susie wanted to know.

"I guess she didn't have any pants on," father chuckled.

Elizabeth looked back, troubled. She still had the feeling they shouldn't have come. The camp was now moving with life again, children and dogs were running down to the beach. But the young Indian hadn't moved yet. He was gazing at them, as if trying to piece together in his mind where they came from, and who Anna was. Anna stared back at him, not speaking.

On the next afternoon, the Sunday, Anna went up to father as he was fiddling with the boat and said, blushing and hesitating: "You show me?" and she went through the motions of rowing.

"You want to learn to row? Why sure! Good idea. . . Hop right in now!" And the children running down saw them out on the lake, Anna splashing this way and that with oars. Once she gave father quite a soaking: he ducked, crying "Ouch!" And Anna's clear rippling laugh echoed back to the shore. Elizabeth danced for joy. "Anna likes it. Anna likes it," she cried.

Every evening thereafter, during the week, when the sunset swooped over woods and water like a great flaming bird, Anna went down to the wharf and untied the rowboat. "Can I come too?" Elizabeth would cry. But both Anna and she knew that mother wouldn't let her; because neither of them could swim. So Anna rowed out alone over the glowing water till she was only a tiny speck rounding Indian point. Then she was gone. And Elizabeth had to go to bed.

On the following week-end Anna would not go out in the boat with father, after supper. Instead she asked mother if she could go to the town to see the pictures.

"What, walk all that way and back again?"

"I like walk. No too hot, nighttime."

After she had gone, father took them all for a canoe ride, to see the sunset. And mother, drowsy amongst the cushions, murmured:

"I suppose it's all right—letting the girl go like that?"

"You should be pleased. It's far better than having her moping. . . It must be pretty dull here for her."

"Not dull at all. It's restful. Anyone should enjoy this holiday," mother said, comfortably.

"For me, anyway. It's a great country! Just look at that cloud!" And, moving carefully so as not to tip, father adjusted his camera with care and precision. The shutter clicked.

"Got it! That'll be a beauty, I'll bet."

Elizabeth smiled; she had heard fishermen speaking in just that tone. But father fished for clouds.

Day followed day in the same pattern; but by August the heat became more intense. The woods were dry and crackling; raspberries hung shrivelled on the bushes and the thrushes ceased their singing. The children quarrelled easily and Anna, on her hands and knees sweating over the bare boards of the kitchen floor, looked flushed and angry. She never talked back to mother but Elizabeth knew she wanted to, sometimes.

That particular burning week-end father brought a friend down with him: and there was much cooking to be done over the hot stove. Elizabeth hung around, helping to beat things; or polishing glasses; trying to peel potatoes. Usually Anna let her help gladly but this Sunday all she would say was "Shoo now! Shoo." So Elizabeth sat on the back stoop, facing the path that led up over grey rocks to the road and watched the sky piling up great clouds. The air was almost crackling. The sun still shone, but it looked sick, greenish. There was going to be a storm, she knew it!

Suddenly there was a commotion in the kitchen. "But I told you not to do it. that way," mother was saying. "I want the potatoes peeled, and scalloped. Like this, see."

"No. No. All cook now," Anna was answering.

"Oh, they're not done yet. Take them out of the oven and start again."

The oven door slammed. Mother went out to the verandah, but Anna began banging pots and pans, clattering dishes. Elizabeth did not dare go inside. And then, in only a few minutes it seemed, mother was back saying: "Oh, I forgot I had this rhubarb the neighbours gave me. Cut it up will you, Anna, and make a biscuit crust for it. That shouldn't take long to do."

"Yes, missis." But there was more banging.

By one o'clock the dinner was ready. Mother rang the brass gong and they all trooped onto the screened-in verandah, overlooking the lake, to eat roast beef on the long oilcloth-covered table. "Whew!" said father. "Must be a hundred in the shade." They all sat hot and sticky, watching him serve the steaming dishes.

"Here, Elizabeth," father said. "Here's Anna's dinner. Just take it out to the kitchen." So she slipped out of the bench seat and held the plate carefully balanced, kicked open the screen door with her foot.

"Anna?"

Anna wasn't in the kitchen. Pots and pans were piled up all over the place. The dipper was lying on the floor. "Anna?" She held her breath, listening. Only the flies buzzed angrily, covering the screen door. Elizabeth set down the plate on the oilcloth, moved back into the living-room and over to Anna's door. She knocked. "Anna?" Still no answer. Usually, at times like these, you could hear Anna crying. But there was not a sound.

Elizabeth turned the brass handle of the rough, unpainted door; she peered round cautiously. Anna's bunk was made up: everything neat as could be. But there were no clothes bulging out behind the cretonne curtain; there were no shoes under the bed. And the worn Polish Bible, beside the soap dish—had gone.

"Daddy. Daddy!" Elizabeth came flying to the verandah. "Anna has left!"

"Left? What do you mean—out for a walk?"

"Surely not." Mother's face flushed. She got up at once. But just then the first flash of lightning sent its tongue lashing against her face. The thunder clapped. And Susie began to cry.

They finished their dinner in the kitchen: for sheets of rain whitened the lake and sprayed through the screen onto the verandah. Elizabeth could hardly swallow the scalloped potatoes: she balked at the rhubarb tart.

Then father went and looked at Anna's empty room. "Well, well," he said.

"You'll have to go out and trace her," mother said.

"In this storm?"

"As soon as it's over."

But there was no trace of Anna, not this day, nor the next. And only Elizabeth guessed, dawdling lonely through the summer morning toward the raspberry patch—only Elizabeth, stooping to find a crushed wet handkerchief on the trail towards Indian Point; only Elizabeth knew where Anna had gone.

First Trials

As long as she could live in her own world, without interference, Elizabeth's relationship with grown-ups was pleasant and easy-going. All day her mother left her alone to play. And Doris, once having got the children dressed and breakfasted, assumed no more responsibility for them. Mother was always busy in the dining-room at her typewriter, with sheafs of green foolscap brought home from the newspaper office, and piles of scribbled notes wandering this way and that across a page. Or she was writing down songs the last Ukrainian servant-girl had sung her; or talking to a Ukrainian minister who came to explain to mother the strangely shaped words. Sometimes the children played around mother in the dining-room, drawing their own paper dolls, colouring and painting them; but more often they were out in the street, and not called until meal time.

It was when she began to go to school that the trouble started. Mother and the doctor had decided, right at the beginning, that Elizabeth was not strong enough to go to school for the whole day. Discussions had to be held with the school principal, permitting Elizabeth to be different from five hundred other children, and attend school only in the mornings. True enough, school did frighten her. The terrible roar of the school yard; the clang clang clang of the bell swung by the principal as if it were a boy he was beating; the rush to be lined up on time; and the difficulty of not answering other children who *would* ask questions after teacher had said: "No talking in line." Then the line moved forward and wound like a snake through bare halls, over a mottled marble floor, and thence to the classroom.

Once in the room, with prayers over and books opened, Elizabeth was happy and excited. She could print already, but here she was learning handwriting; the long addition sums to be copied from the board seemed like a game to her. The only misery was having to go to the bathroom and putting up your hand and teacher not seeing you. Then she had to have another little girl show her the way.

But after lunch, when all the other children were swept back to school, the long lonely afternoon stretched endlessly for Elizabeth, and she would watch the clock for the time when Peggy and Ruby would come racing home to play. Nearly every day she took out her rulers and some chalks and some paper borrowed from mother's pile, and planned how they would play school. Elizabeth was always the teacher. Things worked out well in her head, but as soon as Peggy and Ruby arrived they said they didn't want to play school—they had been at school all day, hadn't they? Elizabeth had set up the small blackboard in the front yard and arranged little chairs in rows. She persuaded her pupils to sit down and do the sums she had written on the board. But all they would do was laugh and joke and whisper to each other, stuffing notes down each other's back and being so bad Elizabeth had to sit Peggy on a dunce stool. She was annoyed at Peggy. Then after a while they would all break loose and start playing hide-and-seek.

Her resentment grew at being kept from the full life of school, a resentment pitched against her mother. This got worse when mother wrote a note to the principal saying Elizabeth was not to be taught writing in the new McLean way, using her whole arm in a free movement. Elizabeth was to be allowed to hold her pencil stiffly between her fingers and write as she pleased. She began to dread going to school and be asked questions as to why she only came mornings and why she didn't have to write like everyone else. She was teased, and her new glasses were pulled off her face, her hair was pulled. At recess Peggy played hopscotch and double dutch with the other girls she knew, but Elizabeth stood by alone; just standing all through recess while hundreds of others shouted, screamed, raced and skipped. At home she began to get into tantrums and to start that nervous twitching of the legs—"stretchiness"—and to be unable to sleep. Finally, mother took her out of school; and from then until she was ten she had a governess who coached her in the mornings, whilst Susie romped nearby.

Grown-ups began to interfere also with the way she looked, the way she walked, the way she dressed. "She's getting all round-shouldered, drooped over a book all day," father would say. And when he took her out for a walk he would repeat, every block or so: "Stick your chin in." She began to think she looked ugly and shrivelled up, a little old woman in glasses. She stopped looking people straight in the eye and buried her nose in a fairy story. Sometimes she wrote out stories herself, or told them to mother to write down. One day mother sent her story to the paper and they printed it on the children's page. "By Elizabeth Longstaffe, aged seven." She was surprised.

Father was more interested however in getting Elizabeth to paint. He noticed her paper doll drawings and her faithful copies of a pear or an apple, given out by her governess to draw. His own family were architects or artists—especially the women. Aunt Appy, at sixty-five, was still painting away like a house afire, striding all over the Isle of Wight to "catch" a picture in watercolours. And at forty, his favourite sister had begun to paint. Father didn't have a boy to plan an education for, so he must have felt Elizabeth's role would be to carry on the family tradition as an artist. He arranged to have her sent to the Art School, on Saturday mornings.

To reach this place you had to go into a queer round building, shaped like a castle, through long halls filled with agricultural exhibits of "No. I Hard Wheat"; and specimens of Manitoba soils; then upstairs to the Art School. The room was white, filled with white plaster arms, heads, torsos and plaques. Sitting at easels in every possible direction were older boys and girls, all with white drawing pads and soft black pencils, drawing away as if they liked it. Elizabeth was given some thick white paper, the kind that crackled, and a smooth pencil. A man found a squeezed-in corner where she could sit on a chair and use a shelf to draw on. In front of her was placed a bunch of grapes—not the real ones, for she had never seen these anyway—a white plaster cast of a bunch of grapes. She was told to draw.

She began copying the grapes, tense and miserable. The air was stuffy, the older children paid no attention to her. No one came near her and as she struggled to put each grape in the right place on her sheet, her head began to throb. By the end of the morning she had a blinding head-ache; she stumbled out into the hall to find Doris who had come for her.

She went two or three more times to the Art School but each time she came home with a headache; mother said it was no use sending her any more.

Father now turned his attention to the way she was dressed. Too sloppy, he said, with her hair always falling into her eyes and her navy blue dress always too big so that she could grow into it. He took her downtown to Eaton's one Saturday morning and said it was time she was spruced up; after trying on several coats he chose one that had a red, white and black check pattern all over it. "Like it?" She nodded, mute. She didn't really care, but it was nice to have father buying some-thing for her and it did look different from the navy blue reefer. She walked out of the store, her head held high.

But when they got home mother cried out in dismay: "Why, Staff, that coat is far too 'loud' for a child. We can't have her going around in that. She'd be so conspicuous." If mother had a rule of life it was not to be conspicuous. She sent the coat back to Eaton's.

From then on father never had anything to say about Elizabeth's clothes; nor indeed about her activities. The world of books became increasingly exciting, something to be lost in, a place where you could forget all the movement of the household, people talking on the telephone, Susie screaming, mother arguing with Doris. She had to be dragged from a book to supper or to bed; for even out in the street, now, her life was restricted. Mother told her the doctor said her heart was not strong enough for her to do any heavy skipping. And so after supper, if she went out, she had to hold the rope while the others did "double dutch." Peggy seemed wilder now than she used to be; she even chased the boys' gang and once when a boy tripped and fell Peggy landed on top of him and kissed him. Elizabeth was shocked.

There was one boy she was thrown up against, whom she had to get along with: David, who shared her morning lessons. He was hard to understand; not because he was mother's friend's son; not because he was so dark-skinned, with heavy thick curls all over his head, like a girl's; not because he was Jewish and the kids yelled at him: "Yaw, yaw, dirty Jew." She had seen them running and chasing him, and she felt a sympathy for him, now that she had been chased too. But she found him hard to talk to; even though she was lonely and wanted to talk he seemed even more far away. Yet when Mrs. Pierce, the teacher, wasn't looking David would tease her, would steal her pencil and hide it. When they were sent out for a recess into the teacher's yard, David never wanted to play tag or jump or do anything she liked to do; he would take out a few marbles and play off in a corner, yet always seeming to watch her out of the corner of his eye, as she skipped or bounced a ball.

She felt she did not like him and wanted to forget about him, yet he would not let her. Crouched there in a corner, his dark curls tossing, he seemed to draw her eyes like a magnet. Yet if she said anything to him he assumed indifference: or else he sneered at the dumbness of girls.

One winter David's parents and Elizabeth's parents decided their children were not athletic enough. Mother probably didn't notice, but it worried father that his daughter did not show an aptitude for games. He found she could not even catch a ball—"butter fingers", he would call her, in exasperation, after playing with her only a few minutes. What she needed was some physical discipline! So it was arranged that Elizabeth and David would spend every Saturday morning taking physical training in a gym class.

The room was in some building downtown. You had to take an elevator and then you came into a narrow hall and were sent into a cubicle to change your clothes. You had to take off your skirt and put on blue serge bloomers—hot and itchy; and take off shoes and stockings and run around the polished floor of the gym, to keep warm. The windows were wide open, even in Winnipeg midwinter, and after exercising all the children lay on mattresses near the windows and practised deep breathing. But the hardest part was running around and around in a circle to music, while someone shouted commands like a soldier and you had to hold your arms high, high over your head till the order changed and then you held them sideways until they nearly seemed to drop off. Then again you would lie on the mattress, breathe the sharp winter air, and swing your legs up as high as they would go.

Neither Elizabeth nor David ever talked about these classes, they were just something they had to go through with which they didn't like. One day, when they were dressing in their cubicles, David called to her from his place, two doors down.

"Hey, Liz! Want to see something?"

"What?"

"Stoop down where the wall ends, and look along here."

Obediently she lowered her head to the floor, wondering what his secret was. When she saw, she stood up quickly, flushing. He was just a rude boy, after all. She did not speak to him, all the way home.

After a few more of the gym classes Elizabeth caught a bad cold and mother found out about lying under the open window, and breathing deeply. Mother told father the exercises were too rigorous for Elizabeth.

As they batted this idea about Elizabeth felt as if she were a ball being tossed between her father and mother. She didn't know who she was. But anyway, there were no more gym classes; and so more time to read books.

The Party

Father was a social man, in spite of his shyness, his stammering, his spasms of irritability. He liked to have people around him. The only trouble was, Winnipeg in those days was like any frontier town. Father was not one of those who danced their Saturday night through by tramping on the money counters of the town's leading bank; he was not in high society. But newspapermen set their own fashion with poker and drink, and it was hard to be convivial without sharing a bottle.

Happily, father had one friend with whom he did not have to drink. Aaron Hoffman was this special friend. Not a newspaperman at all, but an accountant; with a soft, drawling English accent and a voice that was always talking books, books, books. He was tall and thin, very swarthy, with curly dark brown hair and distinguished-looking spectacles. Mr. Hoffman seemed to pay little attention to his charming wife, Wilma; or to his son, David: he would draw father away to his study at the back of the house and the two would only reappear when it was time to go. Aaron would have been perfectly happy in his study for the rest of his

life: but his wife kept urging him to move from the down-at-heels neighbourhood where they had begun their Winnipeg life. She remembered
London and Paris. In Winnipeg, she could never imitate that life of ele-
gance and concert-going; but at least, she said, she didn't have to live in
a dumpy frame house. Aaron could afford something better.

So Aaron was moved to decide on a lot amongst the oak trees, near
the Red River; and once he had started on drawing up plans, with the
help of an architect and many discussions with Jeff Longstaffe, the idea
of a new house became absorbing to him also. He would have it!

Wilma was delighted; and when finally the house was built and ready
for them she sent out invitations to all her friends, for a housewarming.
Wilma Hoffman was a pretty woman, round and soft. Her pale blue eyes
were rather cool, even calculating; but she made up for that with her
carolling English voice. Elizabeth thought of her as "cuddly"—perhaps
because she was so good at making beautiful doll's clothes for the children.
But she was good at making verses too: that made her a special friend
of mother's, and a member of the Women's Press Club.

Mrs. Hoffman had made a special point of asking the children to her
housewarming party. There would be singing and games, she said; and
a little play.

"Can we go, Mummy? Can we go?"

"We-ell", began mother, "it's on a Sunday you know—being Jewish,
Sunday is a different sort of day for them. What about your Sunday
School?"

"Oh, for heaven's sake, skip the Lord for once," ordered father. At
that, Elizabeth and Susie capered; thinking of their new velvet dresses
and of the fur cap and muff that could be worn that day, out into
the dazzling snow.

When that Sunday came, father was late, as usual. He had his breakfast in bed, at noon. Then they had to wait around and wait around
until he had bathed, and shaved, and polished his shoes and made himself immaculate. He could never just put on his clothes and be ready.

Dressing was a ritual, like eating. Time was of no consequence. But at last they were on the way, jammed into the crowded street-car, passing the toboggan slide and rink with scarlet, blue and green toques flashing in the sun; on along Portage Avenue through the centre of the city; and out towards St. John's.

Walking up the broad new steps, painted red, and using the brass knocker instead of a doorbell, hearing the sound of singing within, Elizabeth felt a glow of excitement. Instead of the square box-like sort of house to which she was accustomed, or the huge, mysterious houses of the rich, with their turrets, gables and huge verandahs, this was a New England style of house, so Father said, with green shutters and small-paned windows. "In very good taste," Father said, waiting for the door to open, "but I think Aaron should have taken my suggestion for the door; a broad oaken door would have been much more in keeping."

"Hush," said mother, gathering the girls close to her skirts; and, "Good afternoon, Wilma dear" and "How do you do, How do you do, How do you do" everyone said, as if they had never met before.

"Are we interrupting the concert?" mother said. "I'm afraid Jeff kept us late."

"Oh, not at all," said Wilma; but instead of ushering them upstairs she took their wraps and put them in a hall cupboard and moved them quietly into the long sunny drawing-room. They slipped into some chairs at the back, for there was someone at the piano, and a big girl in a blue taffeta dress stood beside it, singing loudly. Elizabeth was astonished at how high the girl could go and stay there. Then it was David Hoffman's turn to play the violin for them. Elizabeth listened intently. She had never heard a violin before, and the strange squeakiness of the music irritated and yet fascinated her, as did David's dark curly head, his sleepy eyes bent over the bow. But what the children liked best were the games that followed the concert. Musical chairs! Tisket, a-tasket! How Susie clapped her hands at that; how Mrs. Hoffman's mouth rippled with laughter! And finally, for the grown-ups too, post office.

"Oh-h!" With a sudden thump of the heart Elizabeth found it was her turn to go outside, her turn to be chased and kissed. And it was David, who had to choose her, who caught her at the stairs—wide oak stairs that fell like a curve of river, splashed into the hall.

"C'mon."

"No. I don't want to."

"Come on. I *have* to kiss you."

"No!"

"It's the game."

"I don't like this kind of a game."

"It won't hurt you. Just come and get it over with."

"No!" She ran as she saw him coming; and when he caught her arm she had the advantage, above him on the stairs. She pushed, he pulled; and finally in the struggle he slipped, and fell down two or three stairs to the bottom.

"Here, what are you two up to?" It was Aaron, poking his head out of the drawing-room door. "Well, I'll be—" He looked at David, rubbing his cheek ruefully; and he looked at Elizabeth, flushed and triumphant half way up the stairs. A queer light came into Aaron's eyes. "Up man, up! Catch the little she-cat."

"I don't wanta kiss her!"

"What, let a woman make a fool of you? Go after her, man."

"No, I WON'T!" And David had stood up now, was facing his father with that sullen, insolent look on his face.

"Coward!" And to Elizabeth's astonishment, Mr. Hoffman bent down, and very precisely, slapped David right across the mouth. David's fists came up, but his father gave him a push towards the door. "Get back in there, then, if you can't play the game! Sit on the sofa with your mother."

They went through the doorway. Elizabeth stayed on the stairs, suddenly feeling much too hot; her head was stabbing. She didn't want to stay here any more! Finally she stood up, found the stairway zigzagging, wavering before her. She retched; and all the beautiful new oak stairs were soured with Elizabeth's vomit. She crumpled up on the stairs again, weak and crying, until Susie found her and the other strange little girls in their party dresses crowded around—then rushed away, shrieking.

"What's happened? Oh—poor child! Poor girlie!" And as Elizabeth was incapable of saying a word, Mrs. Hoffman led her upstairs and into the bathroom to be washed off.

"The fl-l-oor!" Elizabeth sobbed.

"It's all right, dear. The maid will clean it up in a jiffy. Now don't you worry a bit—see, here's some powder to put on your nose. Ever had powder on your nose?"

"N-no."

"Well, puff, that's the way to do it! Now you look much better. Shall we go down?"

"I just want to—go—home," Elizabeth sobbed.

"All right dear. It's too bad, though, just before supper. But you come and lie down on my bed until your mother's ready—how would that be?"

"All right," said Elizabeth. And lay down on the divan in the soft, satiny room; all fluffed it seemed with pin-cushions and dancing lamps; all soft as sleep.

Elizabeth scarcely remembered going home in the dark, father's arm snug around her; but once she was wrapped in her own hard iron bed her sleepiness left her and she lay tossing, with nightmarish visions of the shining new house, its white trim, soft carpets in a zigzag design, and every room always the same, with the same willow-tree wallpaper. And yet, inside the house, the three strong faces loomed at her larger than life: Aaron so tall and thin with his angry eyes flaming behind the glasses; Wilma almost like a china doll, clinging to her own ways in spite of the battles raging around her; and David, so good looking, but with that dark sneer in his eyes. She didn't like the feel of David, and yet he seemed to be pressing down on her, his eyes engulfing her . . . pushing her down and down. . .

But by next morning, everything had changed. The telephone had rung in the middle of the night and Wilma was on the line crying frantically to father: "Come quick. Come quick! I think Aaron's dead!" And father, trembling and horrified, had jumped into his clothes and hired a taxi and gone off to the Hoffman's new house.

At breakfast he told mother all about it, not noticing that Elizabeth was sitting there, listening. The Hoffmans were all in bed in their own rooms when suddenly Wilma heard Aaron calling from his study: "Wilma! Wilma-a-a!" She ran in to him and found him stretched out, his head fallen over the side of the couch. He was dead of a stroke, the doctor said later. "Must have had too much excitement over his new house."

"Why, I didn't even know he had a weak heart!" father said. "Who would have thought of such a thing? If I had known I wouldn't have argued with him the way I did."

"Oh, nonsense," said mother. "That had nothing to do with it. He liked to argue."

"But I got him excited, you know. He was very excited showing me all over the house."

"The whole day was too much for him. The party. The toasts. . . So foolish," mother said.

"Such a fine fellow—so thoroughly congenial. The only real intellectual friend I had," father said. His voice had grown thin and plaintive, almost like a child's. He went over to the sideboard and poured himself a drink while mother looked on, worried.

"What about the funeral?" mother asked. "Did Wilma make the arrangements?"

"Oh, no, that was all left to the Rabbi. In the middle of the night Wilma said all the Orthodox men arrived, with the Rabbi, and tramped up to Aaron's room and went through some sort of rites and chanting while Wilma lay alone in bed until David got frightened and crawled in beside her. They lay there quaking, unable to sleep, for the tramp, tramp of the feet and the men intoning."

"Poor Wilma," mother said. "Poor Wilma, what will she do now?"

"Oh, she was insured, I expect," father said. "And she never cared about Aaron anyway. She'll have the house. The new house! Ha ha ha!" said father. Then mother told Elizabeth to run out and play and to be very quiet.

It was later in the afternoon that Elizabeth came into the house with Peggy, just to go to the bathroom.

"Zee, Zee!" father called. She looked from the stairs into the drawing-room and there was father, still in his pyjamas. "Come here, Zee, I want to talk to you." Elizabeth cast a scandalized glance at Peggy (what would Peggy say, her father still in his pyjamas?) and signalled to Peggy to go on upstairs. She moved into the drawing-room reluctantly.

Father was sitting on the sofa all red-faced and bleary-eyed; when he talked he didn't look through his glasses directly, but sideways. But his hands pulled her toward him and he began very solemnly: "I want to talk to you. Talk to you. You see, Elizabeth, something very terrible happened to me—very terrible—I've lost my best friend. You know what that means—eh?" She nodded, mute.

"The only person in the world who cared for me—he's gone. Gone out like a m-m-match. Er—ah—" Father's stuttering seemed worse than usual, there would be long pauses between his sentences and he could not get all the words out in one breath. Finally Elizabeth heard the toilet being flushed upstairs and she pulled her hand away from father's. "Did you want me to do something for you, Daddy?"

"Do something? Do? No, no child, there is nothing anybody can do for me—unless you be a friend to me, Elizabeth."

"Yes, Daddy."

"You promise . . . promise you love me?"

"Yes, Daddy."

"Oh, you wretched child!—it's not true, is it? You love your mother best, don't you?"

"No, no! I have to go, Daddy."

"Tell me now, tell me the truth—now which one do you love best—your father or your mother, eh—?"

Elizabeth was frightened; and also impatient. She heard Peggy coming down the stairs. Then there was mother, coming in from the dining-room.

"What are you talking about, Jeff? Do let the poor child go and play."

"Play, play," said her father. "S'all she thinks of! I do everything for her—bring her toys . . . . books . . . . barley sticks—but when I want her she goes and plays."

"Run along!" mother signalled sharply to Elizabeth. And she ran, catching up to Peggy.

Neither of them said anything for a while. It was the first time Elizabeth was aware that father wasn't the same as usual; and that he smelled of drink. Oh, what a smell! She could hardly get enough of the fresh air, here and now. Peggy looked at her strangely as she took in great gulps of air, sitting on the verandah steps.

"Are you going to be sick?" Peggy enquired.

"No. Not *me*! My Daddy's sick." She grasped at that. "You see, in the middle of the night, his best friend died."

"Oh," said Peggy.

Such was the grown-up world. A tangled mass of evidence which the child could not sift; a clash of emotion, of love and hate, with which the child could not sympathize. For her own soul had not opened; love had not reached her. And so she recoiled, drew closer to Peggy, to the street; trying to avoid, at every turn, the strange atmosphere where tall people moved.

Good-bye Daddy

Children are said to be resilient, adaptable. But this is not so. The only reason they move easily is because, like a puppy, they are lifted up bodily by the scruff of the neck, and set down in a new environment. Of their own free will they would never choose to move. For a child's life is essentially static. One place, one time, is happiness. Simply to be *held*. And there is no movement, except within that frame.

Contrariwise, an adult is always conscious of goal. He must be going somewhere; and sometimes this involves a long jump, a new place. The children, of course, are simply expected to adjust to the new pattern without protest and with very little explanation. So it was, when at long last change came for the Longstaffe's, Elizabeth and Susie were not consulted. The fact was given: father was going off to the war, to a place called Belgium.

One thing was clear: father wasn't going to shoot with a gun. He would be safe enough; for he was only going to write, not to fight. But because it was something he had wanted so much, for so long, mother said to Granny that it would be just as well to let him go, even if it came at such a bad time for her. And Granny said yes, the restlessness in him was apparent; and when a man got that way it was foolish to hold him; not that anyone could stop him anyway, Granny said, laughing, once he made up his mind!

The children listened; absorbed the words but did not grasp the meaning of absence; nor did they understand what it would be like to go on a train to Montreal, to visit mother's native Eastern Townships' country, and to see father off at the boat.

The train journey meant little except running up and down the aisles and swinging themselves from seat to seat; until they had to stop to let the conductor go by, or the news butcher, or the ladies going to the toilet. Then at it again swing, swing, and Susie singing at the top of her voice; but getting away with it because of her round, mischievous face and button nose.

Excitement came when they arrived in the strange city, Montreal, so high and narrow compared to the wideness of Winnipeg; and shattered by trolleys clanging, taxis burping and newsboys shouting through their noses the unknown language: "La Presse, M'sieu? La Presse?" All the buildings, though of such solid brick and stone, looked shabby and dirty. The only pleasures to the eye were the park-like squares with long lines of chestnut trees, so huge, so sheltering. But once they were in their hotel at the Place Viger, its coloured chintzes and homey sitting-rooms, with real wood in the fireplaces instead of gas logs; the great height of its French windows and the charm of the chambermaid — these fascinated Elizabeth. They suggested a different world.

"Look what I've found for you!" It was father, dashing into the bedroom that very first day. He was waving in his hands two little wooden cups. "Something for our dollies?" Elizabeth thought; but no, what he was holding proved to be pronged, "Combs! Circular combs!" Father was jubilant. "I was having a shave and haircut in the hotel here — delightful French-Canadian barber, not an anti-conscriptionist at all. At least he congratulated me on the chance to go and fight for La Belle France!"

"But you're not fighting, Daddy!"

"No. But I didn't let that bother me. Well anyway, here he had in his drawer exactly what I have been looking for for years — some scratching combs."

"Jeff!" Mother expostulated; but amusedly.

"But why are they for me?" Elizabeth was realistic.

"To scratch my head, of course. Instead of getting your fingers oily."

"Oh." Elizabeth did not mind scratching with her fingers; father was in the habit, after a long day at the office, of leaning his head back against a chair in the playroom and asking Elizabeth to scratch his head. She did not mind doing it then; but she did not know how it was going to be when travelling. Just when she had got her nose into a new book, probably, father would say: "Scratch!" That was the way it happened today. And rather hastily and snappily she chased the combs around his head pretending they were tanks running back and forth over No Man's Land.

"Thanks old dear. That'll do for now. Keep 'em in your valise, eh, until we need 'em again?" Then for a time father forgot about the combs.

During the hot June days that followed they took a local train away from Montreal into farmland, bordered by beech and maple woods; and then, at the little red station they were met by a sunburnt farm boy, not French at all, who suggested they climb onto his wagon. And wagon it was, with two high benches where you sat, and two spanking grey horses to pull it..."Oh-h!" Susie was frightened; but Elizabeth clambered on with a whoop of joy. Then she heard mother sounding dismayed and: "Oh Jeff, it looks awfully risky for me."

"Can't do you any harm. I'll tell him to go slow." And they were off, down the bumpy white road, the fields soaked in the scent of clover and blue with vetch. Mother forgot her anxiety, pointing out to them the landmarks of her childhood; the "sugaring-off" bush where they had spread maple syrup on the snow, so many springs ago; and the large white wooden houses where the best people had lived — so mother said. Now those United Empire Loyalist pioneers were gone, and a dozen French-Canadian children hung on the fences, staring.

"But it looks just the same, really," mother mused. "It hasn't changed." And Elizabeth, noticing how her voice broke, was startled to see tears in those faraway blue eyes. Elizabeth looked away, quickly.

It was the children's first visit to the country. And Elizabeth wished, fervently, in the days that followed that she wasn't such a city sister; or that she'd been a boy the way Daddy had always wanted her to be. A boy could run, play football, swim as far as father; go on canoe trips and walk for miles and miles. Now, on this special visit to the Quebec countryside, father would spend the first few days trying to toughen up Elizabeth so she could enjoy nature with his own gusto. Against these excursions mother always protested, saying the child was too delicate. And father, irritable, would retort: "You make her so. She needs exercise, that's all the trouble with her." And he thereupon planned, for that very morning, an excursion to the next village. Elizabeth was to walk with him.

They set out gaily. The air was moist with heat; lazy clouds were curled up on the horizon, like little white dogs with their heads tucked in but with their eyes open, watching you. The fields of oats and rye were dazzling, streaming with sunshine. Father, with his walking stick and his camera slung on his back, kept her going at a good clip, talked in a grown-up way of how he had farmed in country like this, with his cousins, when he first came out from England to Ontario. She listened, without breath to answer; pulling her straw hat further over her face; feeling hotter and hotter. She looked far ahead, to the place where the ribbon of road disappeared to the right into a cool green wood; "Is that where it is, Daddy?"

"Where what is?"

"The next village."

"Oh, we've only just started! But there'll be something new around that corner, you'll see." So they plodded on. And it *was* pleasanter at the corner: great maple trees shaded the road; a tiny stream ran alongside, talking to itself.

"Oh-h Daddy! Can I put my feet in?"

"Want to rest for a minute? Very well then." He opened his camera, moved over to a fence on the field side, took aim at a red barn where some cows were grazing. Elizabeth sat at the side of the stream, tangy with pine needles and cool with the arched green of the maples. She took off her sticky sandals, her white socks already stained with sweat; and she put her foot in. "Ouch!" It was cold; but lovely, lovely. The water flowed through her. She dipped her face in it and felt the chill; and then the dry sucking air.

But already father was back, with "Come along now, lazy legs. Why, when I was your age I would think nothing of walking ten miles over the downs, and back again. This will be scarcely five, there and back." Five miles, up hill and down again! The Quebec farmhouses whitewashed, the farms swollen big with barns; calves and piglets to watch, cows browsing, bees humming in the blue vetch along the roadside. Stopping by the ditch for a moment she sank into sweet clover — to see if she could catch a cricket and find out how he chirruped. Instead her eyes fastened on a jewel, surely; a little creature the size of a hatpin head, blazing now green, now blue. Some sort of a beetle, father said.

She could have sat here all day, just watching him climb up one blade of grass, and down another; listening to the cricket's drowsy whirr, like Aunt Maudie's sewing-machine. But father liked walking, when he wasn't taking pictures. He wanted to keep right on.

And so they walked, on and on. Wherever it was they were going, they must have arrived, for she remembered only the return journey, along the same dusty white road, weaving amongst lengthening shadows. This time she saw nothing on either side, her eyes bearing down and following her feet; her legs belonging no more to Elizabeth, but moving beneath her like two sticks; tap tap, tap tap. Funny, to have legs, yet not to know them! But she was to know them that night, for they burned and throbbed right up to the hip and she tossed round and round trying to find an end to the twitching.

"You see," said mother, in the next room, "you walked her too far! I told you she couldn't do it."

"Hasn't she got any stamina at all?" father said, irritably. "Lucky she wasn't a boy — after all. Well, perhaps the next one."

"S-s-sh," said mother. "She'll hear you."

The last memory of that visit to the east stayed with her, even more indelibly. For father was back at the hotel again, in Montreal, slugging away in the heat over a report for the Board, that had to be done before he went to his ship. Mother and the children arrived from the country by train, in time for luncheon. And with unexplained pleasure Ee saw again the wide dining-room, bright with rosy chintz hangings, cloud-white linen glistening on the round tables, table napkins folded with tepees; and the heavy silver sparkling in the sun.

"This one'll be all right." Father stopped the waiter; they all sat down in the middle of the room.

"Couldn't we sit by the window?" mother enquired.

"Eh?"

"I don't like being in the centre of the room."

"Wh-whative y-you s-s-say." Father was stuttering badly. His eyes had that cold, crazy look Elizabeth had come to fear. "Here, waiter! W-w-aiter, can we have another table, eh-over there?"

"Certainly Sir." So the family moved again, picking up handbags and parasols. But once seated there, father objected to the hot sun, and ordered the waiter to draw the curtains. Elizabeth and Susie had already started on a large roll from the other table; they carried these with them and promptly took another roll from the second table. The waiter brought squares of butter in a little silver dish, sitting on ice. Susie took the ice and plunged it into her mouth.

"You shouldn't do that!" Elizabeth frowned.

"Eh, what's that?"

"Never mind," mother said.

"Well what's it to be?" father was looking at the menu. "Chicken broth? or - er-er- how about Crab Louis?"

"No seafood for me," mother said. "I'd just like chicken, thank you."

"Well, Elizabeth can try a Crab Louis - eh girl?"

"I'm sure she won't like it," said mother.

"It's time she tried something besides beef and vegetables!"

So Susie got off with chicken, but Elizabeth was faced with a heaping salad bowl, pieces of pink crab, and a two-pronged fork. While she stabbed away at this, not liking the salty fish flavour, Susie took the paper frills off her chicken leg and put them on her stubby fingers. "Dance to your

Daddy!'' she told her fingers: and kept on with her game all through the meal, much to Elizabeth's disapproval. Then Susie reached the height of bad manners, at the end of the meal when she took the silver finger bowl and instead of delicately dipping her fingers, set the paper frills floating in it like boats. "This is Daddy's ship!" Susie announced, loudly. "Toot-toot. It's going to France!" And mother never even scolded her. Daddy just laughed.

Elizabeth thought they would never leave the table; father sat on and on, even after the finger bowls had been removed; he took out a cigar and puffed hard at it; so the smoke blew into all their eyes and the ashes dripped from his shaky fingers onto the snowy white table cloth. Elizabeth leaned first on one shin, then on the other; twisting the table cloth into her lap and trying to make a doll of it. Father's voice droned on, explaining something over and over to mother, stuttering and sometimes nearly shouting, so that people at other tables looked around; and the tall dark waiter, so like Rudolph Valentino, flicked his eye-lashes.

"I think we'd better go upstairs," mother said finally. So the waiter came and pulled the chairs out and untied Susie's napkin. They moved with flushed cheeks through the long room and out to the hall and up the heavily carpeted stairs to their rooms.

Father sat himself down in an armchair, heavily. The cigar was still in his mouth; but it had gone out.

"Ah-h" he said. "I f-f-eel as if I might have a bit of a nap, eh Zee? How about...how about a s-s-s-scratch, eh old girl?"

"Yes Elizabeth! Do get the combs for him." Mother was lying on her bed, reading. Elizabeth had planned to read the book of Gulliver's travels that Mr. Devlin had given her that very morning. "I don't want to —" she began.

"What, on Daddy's last day? Of course you do!"

So she rose reluctantly from the little chair by the window, went to the adjoining room and found the combs.

"That's the idea — w-w-wonderful idea that was, of mine — a ggreat f-find. Go on girl; harder, if you like. That's the idea..."

Elizabeth stood behind him, her thin arms moving slowly up and down, up and down. Five minutes seemed like an hour; and she tapered off, first dropping one arm to her side, then the other.

"Wha's sa matter? I said s-s-scratch! s-s-scratch my head."

"How long do I have to?"

"Wha's zat?"

"Do I have to keep on?"

"Wha-at? Did I buy those combs for you, or not?"

"I didn't ask you to!" She was petulant, not sensing his mood. For father had sat up, suddenly whirling around to look at her. "You're nothing but an ungrateful child, that's what you are! Just like your mother: whining, complaining. Never giving...Now, get along with it. Scratch!"

Elizabeth backed away. "No," she said. "I don't want to."

"Don't want to! Lillian, did you hear that..!"

"Oh please, Jeff, let it go for now!" But he was aroused now, on his feet; he stumbled, but he seized Elizabeth's arm and shook it, till it hurt. She cried out, the comb dropped to the floor.

"So that's what you think of me, eh? Well I'll show you something too, young lady!" He stooped down, got hold of both combs, threw them to the floor, and ground them to pieces. The thin wood, splintering, whined.

"Oh-h-h!" Elizabeth put her hands to her eyes, turned blindly and ran toward the adjoining room.

"What a shame, Jeff. What a shame," mother was saying, mildly. But father only swore at her, stood up and buttoned his coat and went out the door, slamming it.

"Now you see, Elizabeth!" mother said, loudly enough so she could be heard in the next room. "He'll go back to the bar and be worse than ever."

That night father reported to his ship. The family went with him in a taxi and saw him off at the dark dockside, swarming with men in khaki; with older women crying, young couples hugging. Elizabeth must have been there; but she would never remember saying goodbye.

The Initiation

After their own flat prairie, Oregon was a strange country. Huge hills of sand swooped down, wanting to block the road which somehow kept going, switching back and forth like a whip. Sitting tightly clutched in the fast moving car, Elizabeth was afraid to lean back as mother had told her to. The curves came so suddenly, sucked at her stomach.

That queer feeling ended when the car wheels slowed, sighed softly over a gravel driveway. Under a vault of eucalyptus trees they moved now, a cool tunnel. Then out into the white dazzle of porticoed houses, sloping green lawns. The car drew up grandly, Elizabeth thought, beside high white pillars; the chauffeur opened the door for the three of them and they stumbled out, glad for the feel of pavement, driveway, sound earth.

The door was opened by a uniformed maid; then down the steps with outstretched hand came mother's friend, Mrs. Jellico. "O-o-h!" she cried in her loud but lilting sort of voice: "Such a long journey for these little kiddies. But I'm so glad you could come, dear!" And she kissed mother firmly on the cheek.

"Well," said mother, laughing and pleased, "I only managed the trip because I sold the Encyclopedia Britannica!"

"Without asking your husband?" Mrs. Jellico raised her eyebrows. But quickly hospitable, she added: "I am sure when Daddy comes back from the war he will buy you another one — won't he, ducks?" She addressed the children, and stooped to kiss each one on the mouth. It was a wet kiss, and Susie brushed it off with her hand; but Elizabeth merely tightened her lips a little, constrained by the meeting and the strangeness of this great house, these wide stone steps. They were propelled into a hall as big as the living room at home, with dark floors so polished you could see your shadow in them; and scattered with rugs as bright as pictures. A white balustrade led them upstairs into what was to be Elizabeth's and Susie's bedroom — a vast place. Not a sound did your feet make on the floor because of the thick carpet rich with red flowers. There were two kinds of curtain in the long windows, thick cream coloured lace ones in the middle and heavier ones at the side, of rose satin. Instead of having a blind to pull down, you tugged at a cord and the curtains flew together, changing the room to a mysterious perfumed garden, rosy in the dim light.

After they had had a bath they changed into clean starched dresses. Elizabeth carefully put on her new patent leather slippers that mother had bought her in Portland. They came downstairs, hand in hand, hesitantly moving towards the sound of voices, through a French window and onto a piazza. "Here you are children, just in time for some pineapple juice." Mrs. Jellico handed them a little glass each and "Thank you" said Elizabeth and gulped it down fast, not knowing what it would taste like. Susie stuck her tongue in hers and then spat. Elizabeth frowned, pretending to ignore her, listening hard to pay attention to what Mrs. Jellico was saying about her own children.

"They are just having a visit with Grandma. But I've sent Logan to fetch them home, now that their guests have arrived." Elizabeth wondered if George and Eva would be nice to play with. Of course she knew that they weren't really Mrs. Jellico's children, just adopted; and while they were having a teaparty on the terrace Mrs. Jellico told mother how she had found them. Elizabeth sat on a footstool, listening.

George and Eva weren't even brother and sister, not really. Mrs. Jellico and her husband found George first; he lived with his mother and six bigger brothers and sisters in a tenement house in New York. His mother was a washerwoman and she used to leave George with any old neighbor while she went out to work. His bigger brothers treated him roughly and knocked him about. He never got good food to eat and learned to drink beer while he was just a baby.

It was even more sad about Eva, Mrs. Jellico said. They found Eva in a filthy basement room, with an old blouse covering her, and no pants on. She was eating her dinner on the floor — just crusts which the people at the table had thrown to her. Her body was filthy and her head was a mat of unwashed hair. "But now," said Mrs. Jellico, "you'd never believe it! Her hair is soft, and silvery as the moon." She smiled intently at Elizabeth. "But the poor little thing, children, she never had anyone to hug or kiss her or tuck her up to sleep; she doesn't really know what love is, yet. Why, it was three months before I could get her to smile! And even now you'll see, she's very shy of strangers."

These pictures that Mrs. Jellico had painted with her soft drawling voice grew and glowed in Elizabeth's mind. She could just see the shabby, dirty rooms, the noise of many people living together, the rudeness and loudness of their talk; she could just feel herself shrinking away in a corner, huddled on the floor, hungry for a crust of bread. She felt full of warm pity, longing to take the little girl as Mrs. Jellico had done, and lift her up and hug her and bring her out into the sunshine.

Above her thoughts the women kept the conversation bouncing, mother full of oh's and ah's at Mrs. Jellico's kindness of heart, and Mrs. Jellico interrupting herself only to pour more tea and pass the tinkling cups. They switched from talking about children to talking about books and so Elizabeth moved away towards the edge of the terrace, peering down amongst glossy green-leaved rhododendrons, shrubs and flowers so unreal they seemed to be made of paper and set on a stage. And then, along the driveway, came the purr of the motor; it drew up; again the chauffeur opened the rear door and out jumped a boy, Elizaeth's own size. "Me first, me first!" he was shouting. Timidly behind him stepped a little girl doll, with delicate white face, wide grey eyes; and hair, yes, she had hair like moon-silver.

"Darlings!" Mrs. Jellico rose and ran down the terrace steps to greet them. "George, haven't I told you to wait by the door till the lady steps out? Now wait here, George, no running away till you meet your guests.∴Mrs. Longstaffe, here is my little Eva." She brought the cling-ing child up to mother. "Say how do you do, Eva." But Eva was shy. She kept her eyes on the ground and only much later did she leave her mother's side to join Elizabeth and Susie.

George it seemed wasn't shy at all. He was big for a ten-year-old, with the same silver-light hair as his adopted sister; but his eyes were small, like pale-blue marbles. He got Elizabeth and Susie down to the pool where the goldfish were swimming; then he ran round the rim of the pool, on the nar-row cement, daring Elizabeth. "Bet you can't do this, bet you can't." She started to run the circle, trying to catch him; but he turned suddenly and met her, head on. Instead of catching her he gave a shove — Elizabeth reeled, tottered; a splash, and the icy water was lapping her tummy.

"Oh-oh-o" she spluttered, while Susie shrieked. Elizabeth was too dazed to be angry, but very uncomfortable she was as she dragged herself up onto the cement. George just stood under a tree, snickering, and Susie began to cry. "Come on!" Elizabeth cried, taking Susie's hand and running as fast as she could, with her lovely patent leather shoes squishing with water and her soggy clothes climbing to her middle. The clean starched dress clung flat to her sides like a fish's scales.

"Mo-other! Mo-other!" she bawled, running up to the terrace.

"Elizabeth! Already! You fell in!"

"No — that-boy — he pushed me — he —"

"Was George a little too fast for you?" Mrs. Jellico interrupted; "You must remember dear, he hasn't had opportunities of knowing how to be-have — we will all try and help him, won't we?"

Elizabeth nodded, mute. She turned with her mother and went upstairs to change her clothes, put on her old slippers. When she came downstairs again George was nowhere to be seen. With a sense of relief she began to play ball with Susie and little Eva. Eva couldn't catch very well, but she actually smiled, a shy, flowering smile, when she had run after the ball and thrown it back to Elizabeth. She couldn't throw straight, but this was a hard throw, and it zoomed past Elizabeth and far behind her. Elizabeth chased and the ball ran, down the grassy slope and on towards some bushes. Elizabeth ducked for it, but with a whoop something hurled past her and pounced on the ball before she reached it. George of course.

"Now you don't get it!" he taunted.

"It's Eva's ball," Elizabeth said, with dignity. "You'd better give it back."

"Like hell I will." George bounced the ball, then whirled around and threw it with all his might over the hedge and away, for all she knew, to the road below. Elizabeth wanted to punch him, hard, but she restrained herself and walked slowly back to Eva.

"I can't find it," she said…"Let's play something different. Let's play dollies, eh?"

"Goody, goody," said Susie.

"Has Eva got a doll?" Elizabeth asked, interrupting Mrs. Jellico.

"A doll, is it!" Mrs. Jellico laughed. "I should say she has. Just come to the playroom and see." And Mrs. Jellico led them around the side into another part of the house. She pushed open a door — and there was a room, just like a store — with dolls and elephants and monkeys and teddy bears and boy dolls and baby dolls and dancing dolls — all pinned up in different places to cover the whole wall. Elizabeth and Susie gasped. "There," beamed Mrs. Jellico. "What do you think of that?"

They couldn't say anything; they just looked. Eva didn't seem interested at all, but ran off to a corner of the playroom and fumbled in a box. She drew out a ball, exactly the same as the red and blue ball that had been thrown over the hedge. "Ball — ball." That was the first word they had heard little Eva say.

"We haven't been able to get Eva interested in dolls yet," Mrs. Jellico explained to mother. "You see, she was so deprived, she never had one." Three years old, and never had a doll! Elizabeth was impressed. But what puzzled her even more was how any little girl could possibly choose a doll to play with, if you had what seemed like a whole storeful in your own house. Which one would be *your* doll, your very own? She could not decide, and anyway she did not like to ask that any one doll be taken down to play with — Mummy might think she was "asking." And anyway, the dolls and teddy bears and gollywogs all looked so pretty and satisfied, hanging there on the wall. So after a few minutes of looking the children left the room closing the door softly. The dolls were left behind.

At supper the four children ate by themselves in the nursery, served by Marie, the upstairs maid. She was wearing a green uniform, like a waitress, and she did not talk to the children at all. Soon afterwards little Eva was taken off to bed; and Elizabeth and Susie stood idly by the window, looking out at the wide, pebbled driveway.

"C'mon out," George cried. "Come to the stable and see my pony."

"Have you really got a pony?" Elizabeth had decided not to talk to him, but her curiosity got the better of her.

" 'Course I have...but you can't ride on him!"

"Can I pat him?"

"No, you can just look at Star, while I ride by."

Somehow, the little girls couldn't say no. They joined hands and followed George where he led down some back stairs, out a side door, through a vegetable garden and on towards the white stucco building where the motor cars were kept. Beyond it, from another doorway, George led out a dark brown pony with a fuzzy mane hanging over his eyes.

"Oh, isn't he a darling!" Elizabeth and Susie watched, admiring, as George leaped lightly from stirrup to saddle. First he just trotted around the stable yard, but then he told Elizabeth to open the gate for him: "That big white gate over there." She walked slowly; then fumbled at the latch. "Lift it, lift it!" And just in time, she got the wide gate open; for George came trotting past, gleeful, and out down the long leafy lane.

"Look how far he's going!" Elizabeth looked around towards the house, apprehensive, but there was no one watching. Now they could hardly see where George was riding, the lane seemed so dark with its overhanging cedar branches.

Susie soon lost interest. "Swing me, swing me!" She had climbed onto the white rail gate which Elizabeth began swinging, to and fro. Then they heard mother's voice, and Susie was being called in to go to bed. "Tell her I'm coming too — just as soon as he gets back." Then it was Elizabeth's turn to stand on the lower railing and push herself back and forth with one foot. She was in the middle of a wide swing when she heard hoofbeats again; but before she knew it George had trotted up with such force that pony and rider lunged into the gate. Elizabeth was swung wide, lost her balance, and tumbled off onto the ground.

"Ow-ow!" she cried out, but trying not to cry. George dismounted, flung the reins over the gatepost, and stooped to pick her up. "Gee! Are you all right?"

"I guess so." She shook herself, shivering. Then she found that her left wrist was scratched and bleeding.

"You go on to the house...there, the kitchen door! The cook's got bandages." So saying, he gave her a little push. Then he clambered onto Star's back again, wheeled, and was off down the lane at a canter.

By the time Elizabeth reached the house, she was sobbing. But her wrist was bandaged and she was taken by Marie up to bath and bed. "Oh dear, oh dear," mother said, sitting down on Susie's bed to hear her prayers. "And spank that bad bad boy!" Susie concluded. Elizabeth, too tired to talk, fell asleep to dream that George was being kicked downstairs by his big brothers, and whacked by his big sister, Elizabeth.

In the morning the soft rosy light beckoned her. She got up noiselessly, not to wake Susie, pulled on her clothes and went across the hall to the shining white bathroom. Then she found her way to the top of the carpeted stairs. She was just starting down when "Swoop!" and from behind who could it be but George, sliding past her down the bannister.

"H'lo," said George, looking up at her.

"H'lo," said Elizabeth, out of sheer surprise.

"Want to slide down?" he asked her, his small blue eyes guileless.

"I'd better not," she said, with dignity, remembering her bandaged wrist. Still, it didn't hurt any more. She hesitated, looking down at the delightful curve of the bannister.

"You slide down and I'll catch you — honest I will!" He crossed his heart and spat.

"No. You'd just go and hurt me."

"I would not! Honest...How was I gonna know your arm was so strong, nearly breaking that old gatepost?"

"Did it?" Then she saw he was joking. She began to smile and George began to laugh and she nearly laughed too.

"Don't you know how to slide?"

"'Course I do. I can do anything."

"Sure you can. C'mon. Slide down quick, before anybody comes."

Elizabeth lifted one leg over; grasped the handrail; and in a moment was flying down the bannister, sheer joy, down and down to George. This time George was ready; he did catch her. But her weight knocked him over and the two of them rolled together onto the bright Persian rug. Breathless, they began to laugh, a mass of heaving arms and legs, rolling and laughing.

"GEORGE?" Mrs. Jellico's warning voice came echoing down from some uncertain place upstairs.

"Hurry!" George whispered. "She'll catch us. Let's run! I'll race you to the stables."

And Elizabeth ran.

Father's Boy

The year that father was overseas as a war correspondent was the year that mother took off "on a spree" and travelled to the West Coast to visit relatives. It was the first long train journey for Elizabeth and Susie; and their first view of the ocean.

When they returned to Winnipeg, it was July. Elizabeth moved into the deep of summer, the sun a great friend streaming warmth into her bones. And across the street there was Peggy come flying, her eyes more like cornflowers than ever as she opened them wide to hear the tales of Elizabeth's travels.

"And mother says," Peggy confided, "that I can invite you soon to come and spend the night at my house."

To sleep at Peggy's house! Elizabeth tingled; she felt a little aghast, but encouraged by Peggy's evident delight. She had never been away from her parents at night, unless it was at Granny's house.

Suddenly the special evening came. Susie went off on a visit to Granny's. Mother packed Elizabeth's night-gown in a little bundle and gave it to her, with her tooth-brush. "Good-night, dear. Have a nice time at Peggy's."

"Yes, mother." Elizabeth stooped obediently to kiss her mother, who was in bed herself. Mother had been sick ever since they got home from the West. "Be a good girl," mother said.

She nodded. She found Peggy on the front steps, impatiently waiting for her. "Mother said when it gets to be dusk, we can go to bed. Won't it be fun?"

They crossed the street, arms wound around each other's waist. When they got to the Green house there was no one on the verandah; and no one in the living-room or kitchen.

"They've gone already," Peggy said.

"Gone?" Elizabeth was puzzled.

"Gone to a show. But they'll be back, you know. Mother said we could each have an orange and eat it in bed—see, here's my big bed out on the back porch!"

Elizabeth had never been upstairs in Peggy's house before. Mrs. Green didn't usually like Peggy to bring her friends in. Now Peggy had a friend to stay the night, but there was nobody to look after them! Elizabeth felt a dull cloud gathering in her heart.

"Maybe we shouldn't go to bed, " Elizabeth said, "until your mother comes home."

"Sure we should, that's what mother said we should do. Let's race eh? I bet I'll be undressed before you." Peggy shook her nut-brown curls and began to undo her white button boots.

Elizabeth undid the buckle of one sandal, then the other. Doubtfully, she opened the paper bag and pulled out her night-dress.

"Oh, it's pretty, a pink one. Yours is pink, mine's blue!" And Peggy pulled her nightie quickly over her head, and giggled as she got caught in it. "Help! Help! Let me out." Elizabeth laughed too, Peggy looked so comical. But then her face sobered. She folded up her nightgown again.

"I think I'd better not stay," she said. "I better go home."

"Oh, no-o-!" Peggy was incredulous. "You can't do that, Elizabeth!

What would mother say? You're invited to stay."

"I don't think my mother would like it. There's nobody here to look after us," she said stiffly.

"Why, I'm often alone. Or me and Jack, we're often alone while Dad and Mum and Rita go somewheres. It's safe as safe."

"What if a burglar got in, downstairs?" Elizabeth challenged.

"All the doors are locked."

"I know, but Will—I mean, a boy got in our house and stole my bank. Burglars don't get in doors, they get in windows." She looked apprehensively towards the windows of the porch, all screened in.

"We never had a burglar," said Peggy. That settled that. "And you can't go home, Elizabeth, you just *can't*! Your mother wants you to be here."

"Why does she?"

"I dunno. She just does. My mother says there was a doctor coming to your house tonight."

The doctor! A chill seized her. What if mother were very sick—what if she died? Elizabeth felt the tears forming in her throat.

"I got to go. I just got to go. I'm awful sorry, Peggy. . . I'm going right home now!" And as Peggy lay in her nightie saying mad things and then crying too, Elizabeth got her sandals buckled again and left, running down the stairs fast, unbolting the front door, away across the street into the hurrying dark.

She found mother in bed, with the blinds drawn. A nurse in a white uniform was bustling about.

"Why, Elizabeth! What's the matter?"

Elizabeth sat gingerly on the bed, to make sure mother was just the same. She tried to keep the tears back. "There was nobody to look after us," she explained. "Mrs. Green's out. . . Mummy. Do I have to stay there? Can't I sleep in my own bed?"

"Oh, I suppose so." Mother stroked her hair. "There, kiss me; and go right off to sleep now—no imaginings." Elizabeth looked at the nurse; she swallowed.

"I'll go right to sleep, Mum, honestly I will!" And for once she did.

When she awakened it was broad daylight. The shadows of people walking along the street were reflected on her ceiling, slow steady shadows whom she dressed up in her mind's eye, dreamed about. There was the thin man, hurrying off to work; and now the scrub lady; next the princess. . .

A sound broke in upon her story-telling. A strange sound, something like a cricket—no, a crow! squalling. Her heart began to beat fast, she held her breath, listening. "Ah-ah-ah" it quivered again.

"Mother!" she called, still in her bed. "Mother!"

"Are you awake, dear?" called mother, very happy. "Come and see the baby doll I've got for you—in your doll's cradle."

She had a swift picture of the dimity doll dress wrapped in mother's trunk. No, it couldn't be that. She knew now! She knew what she would find as she put a bare foot on the floor, felt around for her slippers. Nearly bursting with shock she tiptoed into mother's room.

The blinds were down still and the room had a greenish half-light, with the gold sun peeking in through chinks and cracks. There lay mother in the wide bed; and right beside the bed, on the floor, was Elizabeth's doll cradle, the one Willie had made for her.

"Come and look," mother smiled. Elizabeth bent over, peering in among the soft flannel blankets. All she could see was a tiny puckered red face, a sweep of fine black hair. Then the eyes opened, blue as Peggy's. . . The little creature squalled, right into Elizabeth's face.

"Oh," she said, nearly crying; yet laughing too. "It's a brother!" mother said. "A baby brother for you, Elizabeth."

"A boy?"

"Yes."

"Can I hold him?"

"Yes. Lift him up in the shawl, see—very gently now; there, just like a doll, isn't he? Tiny as a doll."

She held him for a moment, a wave of feeling surging between her and the bundle. Then the nurse came in and Elizabeth was shown how to tuck the baby up again in his nest.

"Mother?"

"Yes, dear." Mother sounded tired.

"Is that why Susie went to Granny's and why I had to go to Peggy's?—
Why didn't you tell me?" She was choking, puzzled, yet happy too.

"We weren't sure he would live, dear. The doctor said he might be
born dead."

"Oh. . . Well now he's alive, I guess Daddy'll come home quick, won't
he?"

"We'll send him a cablegram. He'll be so excited about having a son!
But he won't be able to come home, not yet awhile."

"Not even to see his boy?"

"No. Because the war is on."

The nurse began fussing around mother's bed and Elizabeth was told
to run along now and go down and have her breakfast. Aunt Maudie
would be there to look after her.

"Well, how do you like having a little brother, Elizabeth?"

"I don't know." She stuffed a spoonful of porridge in her mouth and
seized a piece of toast as she heard the doorbell ring. It was Rita, come
flying over to see mother. And after her came Peggy.

"I know what you've got!" Peggy said, her eyes saucer-sized.

"I bet you don't." Elizabeth was baffled; she did not know whether she
was supposed to tell anyone about this new arrival.

"I do so! Can I see it?"

"What d'you mean?"

"What you've got upstairs."

"No. I'm supposed to go out and play."

"Oh." Peggy was disappointed. She sulked, and said she wouldn't play.
She'd go right back home, so there. But before they got into a fight about
it, Aunt Maudie appeared in the doorway. She was astonished that Elizabeth hadn't told her friend the great news. "Why, if I had a baby brother
I'd be just bursting to tell everybody on the street."

Elizabeth did not bother to explain that she thought it was a family secret, not to be told to the neighbours. It had been kept secret even from Elizabeth. But now everything was all right, you could talk about it. She squeezed Peggy's arm. "C'mon, let's go over and play at your place."

"Can I see him soon, d'you think?"

"Maybe, when the doctor says so. He's coming back today."

"Oh, isn't it just lovely! I guess the doctor brought him last night, in his bag," Peggy began, as they crossed the street.

"I dunno." Elizabeth had other ideas, not to be divulged to Peggy. Sometimes Peggy seemed awfully silly, like now when she was chattering and chattering of how the baby brother would be a great thing for her brother, Jack, to play with.

"But why Jack?"

"Because Jack's lonely, he has no one to play with."

Elizabeth was doubtful. "But my brother is only a baby. He's too young to play with Jack."

"Oh, they grow up fast—before you know it," Peggy said, blissfully. And she took Elizabeth through her gate and into the back garden, where they cooled themselves by lying under the rhubarb plants—the huge leaves like elephants' ears, fanning their faces.

After lunch Elizabeth tiptoed upstairs as Aunt Maudie had told her to do, quietly; past the bedroom where mother was sleeping, and softly turned the handle of the bathroom door. That was where the doctor had ordered the baby to be—in the bathroom, snug inside his cradle, with a heater in the room to warm him. He was so small, the doctor said, it was a miracle he had been born alive. So nobody had expected him, and nothing was ready for him except Elizabeth's doll cradle.

She opened the door a crack, then crept in. There he was, just a snug bundle with a puckered-up red face. He was asleep. She gazed for a moment, then slipped out again; full of dreams now, like Peggy's. She would not have to take Willie Weeks out any more, she had a brother of her own to walk down the street with!

Next morning Susie came home, along with Granny; the clergyman came too, Mr. Goodall; and Elizabeth was called upstairs to come and hear the baby being christened. His name was to be Richard.

Elizabeth and Susie knelt down near Granny in mother's bedroom; but when the long prayers started Elizabeth felt the room too stuffy, and the praying too much like in church. She tiptoed out and ran downstairs to sit on the front steps. She could hear Mr. Goodall's voice droning on from the upstairs window. She felt much more comfortable where she was, though a little ashamed for having run away.

Mr. Goodall finally came down and passed her on the steps, patting her absently on the head. At the gate he turned, realizing who she was. "You should have stayed for the service," he said. "You should do what your mother says, not always having your own way."

Elizabeth flushed, darkly; she wanted to shout a taunting rhyme at him; but luckily for her, Susie arrived clattering down the steps and the house was again filled with the sound of voices, all released and happy now because the baby had become Richard and he was safe in the doll cradle.

That afternoon Elizabeth still felt full of excitement, with dreams of yearning to rock the baby in her arms. She tiptoed up to the bathroom and peeked in. The baby hadn't cried for a long time and the red of his face seemed bluish. She poked him. He did not stir. Frightened, she ran downstairs quickly and slipped like a ghost out into the sunshine.

"Elizabeth!" Aunt Maudie's voice wakened her from a sleep she had fallen into, on the lawn. "Elizabeth! Mother wants to see you."

Her heart pounding, her mouth dry, she climbed the stairs. The room was darkened again. Mother lay with swollen breasts. Her eyes were all red-rimmed, her voice was shaky. "I'm sorry to tell you, dear, the little baby has gone."

"Gone?"

"Yes, the doctor came and took him away. He had always said the baby would not live." Mother's voice cracked, the tears streamed down her face.

"You mean—Richard's dead?"

Mother just nodded. She couldn't speak any more, the tears were running so fast down her cheeks. Mother crying! Elizabeth had never seen her mother crying before. She could not bear it, but turned and ran from the room. Through the open door of the bathroom she could see her doll's cradle, the blankets all disturbed. The cosy nest was empty.

So father didn't get his boy, after all.

The Other Side of the Street

That day Elizabeth was trading "samples" with Peggy Green on the front steps. Spread out before them were old cardboard chocolate boxes full of tiny samples, miniature soaps and perfumes that father asked for whenever he went into a drugstore. Direct morning sunshine brightened the trade. In the shade it would have been a quieter business, slow and cool. Instead, words were getting sharp. Her friend Peggy said:

"Well, then, I'll give you my palmolive and the zambuk for that new toothpaste tube."

"Both of them?"

"Uh-huh."

Elizabeth's arm moved. Gingerly, she picked up the toothpaste tube. She held its cool roundness, weighing its worth. And there, in the back of Peggy's box, she saw again that darling wee bottle of green perfume. She remembered yesterday's violent quarrel—

"I know what, Peggy!"

"What?" Peggy raised her eyes, cautiously.

"I'll give you the toothpaste, *and* my lilac powder tin—if you'll trade for that little perfume bottle."

"No," said Peggy.

"Aw, come on, Peggy, please! We can always trade it back again."

"When?"

"Oh, anytime."

"Tomorrow?"

"Maybe tomorrow. Aw, come on. Please, Peggy."

The barter was balanced there, almost ready to tremble in her favour. And then didn't Rita Green, Peggy's big sister, come and spoil it all. From the house across the street she came running; she pelted through the gate, letting the latch click behind her.

The little girls thought that Peggy must be called home. "Aw, do I have to go?" Peggy pouted. But Rita ignored her, ran past them both up these steps; and then through the open doorway into the dark hall, her pigtails flying. Rita was crying.

"What's the matter with Rita?" Elizabeth asked Peggy, leaning down in a whisper. Their trading was suspended. The cold cloud had come over Peggy's face.

"Oh, I guess it's just mother and Rita—they fight all the time. Rita cries. Rita wants to go in for being a nurse, but mother won't let her."

"Why not?"

"How should I know?"

"It would be nice to be a nurse," Elizabeth suggested conversationally. But Peggy didn't want to talk about it so she said nothing more. But upstairs, from the open window above the verandah, she could hear the low hum of voices. Rita was with mother, telling her troubles to this side of the street.

It had all happened before. Rita shouting an angry word to her own mother, Mrs. Green, and banging out of her own house; running across the street as if she really believed she lived in this house. It was wrong, somehow. Granny had said it was wrong, hadn't she? Telling mother she shouldn't interfere with the neighbours, no matter what trouble they were in. But mother lying upstairs sick all these weeks, with nothing to do, and Rita having no one who could understand how much she wanted to break away and try for a nurse; somehow Rita just had to come and talk to mother. But it seemed to upset things, to put a great black cloud between this house and the house across the street.

Long after the screen door had banged shut the two little girls sat in silence on the verandah steps. Elizabeth hardly dared look at Peggy; instead she fiddled with her samples; then scattered them roughly away.

"Aw, let's not play this any more," Peggy said. "Come on, let's skip!" Peggy picked up the rope and began chanting. "Blue bells, cockle shells—" but Elizabeth didn't feel like skipping or singing. She watched Peggy flipping the rope in flashes over her head. Then the twelve o'clock whistle blew, startling them.

"Guess I gotta go home for lunch." Peggy began picking up her samples, not without a quick glance at the upstairs window.

"Well, g'bye."

"G'bye." Peggy shrugged her shoulders and ran out across the street.

Then Elizabeth, too, moved indoors. It was cool and quiet. In the dining-room lunch was ready, and mother was actually downstairs, sitting across the table from Rita.

"Hello, dear. The doctor said I could come downstairs today, for a little while."

Elizabeth slid into her place, saying nothing. Rita Green was silent also, her red eyelids lowered upon the plate of macaroni and cheese. But mother was busy. In between bits of macaroni and white bread-and-butter mother leaned over to where the telephone hung on the wall. She clutched at the receiver, calling numbers that she had torn out from the newspaper jaggedly, with her hairpin.

"Hello?—Yes, in answer to your ad—are you suited? No, it is not for myself. A young girl I know is anxious for a position. Yes, she is very good with children. . . Seventeen. . . Oh, very clean and competent."

Rita winced. Rita still kept her eyes lowered, pretending to eat, but not eating. She was really just listening, listening to the words on the telephone, her breath held in as if it got in the way of her hearing. Yet mother's voice was high-pitched, loud and sure. Mother was trying to get Rita into somebody else's home. Away from her own home across the street. Away from Peggy.

Suddenly Elizabeth couldn't eat any more, either. Cornstarch pudding, on top of the macaroni and cheese, seemed too difficult a task. When mother had laid down the telephone and turned to her cup of tea, she asked: "Please, Mummie, may I be excused?"

"Why yes, dear." Mother seemed relieved to have her go, not noticing the untouched pudding.

"That one sounds like a good place." Mother began talking quickly to Rita.

Elizabeth went outside again, looked longingly across the street. The early afternoon swooned in the heat, dragged on; still Peggy did not come out to play. She was sure Peggy must be at home, but the house on the other side of the street had its blinds drawn down to keep out the sun. It looked forbidding, as if only pretending to be asleep. At the least stir or poke, she thought, the eyes of Peggy's house would flash open, their hard light shooting through you. No, the eyes of that house had better be left alone, like the eyes of Peggy's mother. . .

On the sidewalk in front of her own house Elizabeth began to play hopscotch by herself, lazily, without enjoyment. Then suddenly her heart skipped as she heard Peggy's front door opening. Out they came, Peggy and Mrs. Green. Peggy had on her pink dress, newly starched, and her flowery sun-bonnet. She must be going downtown with her mother.

Out of the corner of her eye, she watched them flounce down their steps, pass by the low green railing they called a fence, then turn towards Portage Avenue. Peggy seemed to notice her, but didn't dare wave a hand. She bobbed along the street beside her mother, who took quick hard steps away from the house. Then, tossing her arm upward with a snap, Mrs. Green let her dark green parasol envelop them both.

Almost immediately from above the verandah a blind snapped upward. Mother's bedroom was awake again. She could not have rested very long!

The low voices started again. Then silence. Presently quick steps sounded on the stairway and Rita came out of the front door in a great rush. She slammed the gate, making it click resoundingly like Granny's false teeth.

"Hi, Rita," she called to the big girl, tentatively. But Rita was already crossing the street to her own house. Rita tripped, and nearly fell into the pile of manure that lay fresh and unmashed on the curb. Fascinated, Elizabeth followed, sneaked towards the road to look. The milkman's horse had probably done it, while he stood nibbling the few sparse leaves of the boulevard tree. Poor thin little tree, she thought, beginning to feel the ache in her side. Poor little tree that never seemed to grow. Often she would have liked to push away the horse from gulping at the tree, but his huge glittering eyes frightened her. The driver never cared, even if his horse stepped right over the curb and onto the grassy boulevard. . .

Now Rita had picked herself up, was heading for the side door of the Greens' house. Under a mat a key would lie hidden.

"Hi, Rita! Your mother's gone down town," she shouted.

"Shut up," Rita's lips said, as she tossed her pigtails. But she must have been whispering, for the words made no sound. All the same, they bounced hard against her face. They made Elizabeth turn back into her own garden, fast.

What did she care anyhow if Rita Green was going to get heck? Rita had never cared for her—nor for Peggy, either. It was as if the big girl had cobwebs on her face, and kept stroking them aside, trying to see the world. Elizabeth was much smaller, but she could see the world clearly, the flawless sky, the sunshine a great golden roof vaulting the street. Nothing on the pavement but hot white light, ribboning the dull boulevard. Nothing moving. Only in the hollow concrete ditch near the sewer, some sparrows were having a dusty bath.

She sat down on the garden grass, trying to look for four-leaf clovers. She would be alone now, all day. No one to play with. Soon Rita would be coming out of the house across the street, quickly like a thief. Yes, there she was, straw hat on her head; old leather suitcase pulling her sideways as she struggled with it to the street. Then, when Rita reached the green railing she put her burden down for a moment, looked up towards mother's bedroom window and waved a gloved hand.

Elizabeth could not see her mother. She was lying inside the garden on the grass, pressing its dampness into a round nest. If she lay back, head on her arms, she too could get a squint up at the window. Yes, mother was sitting there, smiling but a little tearful. Her hand gave Rita a quick little wave. Cocky, mother seemed to be; yet underneath, not sure of herself. If *she* felt that way, it was because she had been bad. If *she* waved her hand like that, it was rapped sharply with a pencil.

But mother waved her hand and Rita nodded, very quickly as if someone might see her. Then she hurriedly picked up her suitcase, reeled around the corner. She was heading the opposite way, towards the park. She disappeared.

The afternoon hung so quiet now, it seemed to have stopped breathing. Rita was gone, and her own stomach had pain in it. Rita was gone; and Peggy would be gone too, never allowed to play with her any more. She knew. She *knew*. Best thing to do now would be go down the next block, across the street, down the lane, and see whether the Schulz kids were out playing. She moved that way slowly, but there was no one in sight. And so she hovered back and forth all day, not knowing which way to go, what to do. All the while her left side had a dull ache in it, full of the feeling of Rita; she wondered what Rita would be doing tonight, in a strange house. And so, to forget it, she would pick up her skipping rope and try skipping to a hundred, faster, faster. That was how she came to be out in the lane, still playing, when the cool of evening came. That was when Mrs. Green's flapping arms bore down on her.

"Well, child, where's my daughter—Rita?"

"I don't know." The hung head, the pounding heart.

"But you saw her go, didn't you?"

Silence.

"Didn't you? Didn't you? Tell me, you little imp!" Peggy's mother had an awful temper. She seemed to be near to grabbing her, shaking her.

"Yes." A scared gulp.

"Where did she go then?"

"I don't know." Her head hung, she felt the guilt and shame upon herself.

"You don't know?" The woman was nearly screaming. "But Peggy says you saw her. Rita was talking to your mother."

"You'll have to ask my Mummie."

"Your mother is supposed to be sick—not to be disturbed. But if she's been interfering with *my* family, I'll see to her, I will!"

Elizabeth stood there, paralyzed. Then suddenly it was over. The door slammed as Mrs. Green went into their house by the side entrance, dragging Peggy with her.

She turned and ran. Only as she drew near her own side of the street did she begin to lag a little. What was there to go home for? She opened the gate, hesitant, heard it click behind. There ahead of her on the steps lay the scattered "samples", never put away. She began to pick them up forlornly. The brightness of the morning—where was it? She looked upwards, loving always to look for the twilight creeping on, drawing veils over the face of the sky. But tonight the dusk came down fast, like a chill blind. . .

It covered the street, and the other side of the street. And she couldn't see the house across the street any more.

The End of a War

If it hadn't been for father's letters "from the front" where, as Elizabeth had learned to say, "My Daddy is a war correspondent", the children would not have noticed the war very much. Without radio or television, with only black headlines in the Free Press, war did not seem important unless one was at Granny's house, watching her search those columns marked "Killed in Action" or "Missing." Or else war meant a parade, a Scottish bagpipe band, and young men with bright faces marching along Portage Avenue, their kilts flying.

Father's letters, too, seemed to make war an exciting, happy kind of a picnic. After supper, if a letter had come that day, mother would read the children "bits" written especially for them.

"It is rotten luck not to have my girls—my three girls, here, but except for that I am very happy and having a lovely time.

"I have what we call a bedroll and inside is a warm sleeping-bag like a double duvey. Sometimes I sleep in a tent on the ground (and that is the best fun of all) but the past few nights I have had a real bed and mattress in a real house. My, what luxury! Next door is a pretty garden with roses just like in Victoria. On the other side is a small cottage and in it are two little girls, Annette and Pauline. 'Here is half a franc, my little children,' I say; 'Merci, Monsieur, thank you, sir,' they answer, and smile nearly as prettily as Peggy when she says she won't take ten cents but wants to very badly all the time. By the way, how is Peggy? Sometimes I look up in the sky and see her eyes and I look over the fields and see her hair—but I never hear her laugh, because the children of France do not laugh. They are sorrowful little children. Annette's and Pauline's father was killed in the war—'Many years ago, Monsieur'—by which they mean 1914. It is a long time to be without a father. Their brother is just seventeen and he has gone into the army. Their mother is working in a munition factory a long way off. They live with their grandmother—or perhaps their great-grandmother—she looks at least a hundred. There is no school here—the teachers went away when the Germans came so near. But now the Canadians have driven the Germans a long way off and school is open again. Always remember, dear girls, that it is our Canadian boys who won this great victory. If the people on each side of us had kept up to us we should have been at the Somme river on the fourth day (Sunday). I am going to draw you a map which I think you can understand. You will see how much further the Canadians went than anyone else. . . There are no soldiers in the world equal to our Canadian boys and if we had a lot more of them nothing could stop them. We think we are on the way to Berlin."

But the children did not quite understand these messages and only really listened when father wrote, "I suppose when I get back you will be so tall and fat that you can't ride pig-a-back any more. 'Ugh! Ugh! Ugh!' That is Big Bear. 'Run, children, run, or he'll get you'. "

Those games seemed very far away now. But maybe, maybe, Granny said, the war would end soon and the fathers would come marching home. Meanwhile, here in Winnipeg, this was November, the grey season: no snow, not very cold. They had left their own street, their own house—rented now, for the duration—and were stopping at Granny's before moving to a rented apartment. Elizabeth was out playing, in the middle of a grey morning, when suddenly a mill whistle shrieked; then another! and another! until they were all baying like hounds. Neighbours rushed out onto verandahs, then down to the gate as if they could see, up the street, what the whistles were blowing about.

"Why it must be—! The war must be over!" Granny's neighbour burst into tears and ran back into her house. Elizabeth caught the excitement, spurted up the steps and into Granny's door.

"Mummy! Mummy!" Mother was at the telephone in the hall. "Mummy, Daddy's coming home! The war's over!"

"Yes, I heard it, dear." She put the receiver back on the hook. "That's what everybody says, Elizabeth, but it's just a rumour. I've phoned the office and they say it isn't true."

Not true! Elizabeth was crestfallen. Not true, and yet everybody was believing it! She turned and went outside again, to prove it to her own eyes. People were streaming into the street. She followed them a little way towards Main Street and saw that the stores had mysteriously brought forth flags, balloons, whistles and horns. Grown-up men and women grabbed at coloured streamers, laughed and threw confetti. The march began to the City Hall.

Elizabeth ran home this time, certain the war was over. "Gee, Mum, there's going to be a big, big parade! Can't we go? Can't me and Susie go?"

Mother explained that she had different plans. This was the day they had chosen for the family to move to the rooming-house. Elizabeth knew, didn't she, that their own house was leased and all the goods and furniture had been sent on to the new address, in St. James. She told Elizabeth they would be going soon, on a street-car.

"Take a taxi," Granny urged. "You'd be safer in a taxi." So mother phoned and phoned, but she could not get a taxi. "Humph," said Granny, "Commandeered."

"It's ridiculous," said mother. "The war isn't over!" But Elizabeth had only to go outside and listen, to hear the war being over. A lump formed in her throat as she heard the far-off tooting and shouting. If only they could be there, too, waving and shouting! But it was no use. Mother was going to move.

Later they did get to the corner of Main Street, carrying bundles and with mother holding the suitcases. On the platform they had to wait and wait until a street-car came, not too loaded to get on. They stood together, jammed into the front of the car, while people all around loomed heavy and thick with excitement, towering over the children, stepping on their feet as they shouted, sang and blew loud on cardboard trumpets.

Even above the din Elizabeth could hear mother saying, in a high voice: "Such nonsense. The war isn't over! There's no official word to that effect."

"You're crazy!" a man shouted. "Of course it's over. Hooray! Hooray! Hooray! The war's over. Bring the boys back home."

"Bring the boys back home!" the street-car chanted.

"Bring the boys back home," Elizabeth prayed, under her breath. They had to get off at Portage and Main, to transfer. Elizabeth and Susie clutched mother's skirt, one on each side, as they wriggled their way off. Then Elizabeth tugged:

"Please, Mummy, can we have a horn?"

"Toot too-ot," said Susie.

"No," said mother, cross. "There's nothing to blow for. The war is still on!" And she marched ahead while Elizabeth and Susie tried to keep up, wading through the thick muddy pool of people. Elizabeth saw the streamers catching in mother's wide-brimmed hat, a balloon going off in mother's face, horns blaring in her ears. "Hooray! Hooray! Hooray! The war's over!" the crowd thundered.

Elizabeth and Susie watched as mother drew them close to her and took her stand on the next platform and signalled wildly for a street-car to stop. It rolled on. Then another. And another. Above their heads flags were waving, horns too-tooting. Elizabeth longed desperately to have, if not a horn, just one little flag—one of those little silk flags on the black stick. But mother said no.

Finally a street-car stopped. They squeezed on, somebody lifted Susie over his head onto the back platform. And that was as far as they could go, jammed to the outer platform and stuck there, scarcely able to breathe. "Hip-hip hoor-a-ay!" came the hoarse roar of the people. People whom Elizabeth couldn't be a part of, must move with, and yet be separated from.

"You're all foolish," mother shouted to those around her. "My husband is a war correspondent and the office says there is no official news at all. It's a false rumour. The war is *not* over."

"Boo! Boo! Boo!" shouted the people, as the street-car swayed and rocked. Elizabeth felt dizzy, a sick empty feeling in her stomach. She tried to hide her face in mother's skirt so people would not notice her; so they wouldn't wonder why she too wasn't a part of this great moving mass of humans, swaying and singing, deliriously happy, chanting those words: "Bring the boys back home!"

At last they had left the roar of the city centre, they were coasting along into the quiet of St. James. Mother pulled a bell and they struggled off the car. Elizabeth felt bruised and bumped and terribly glad to be breathing the fresh November air.

"Are we here now?" asked Elizabeth.

"Yes, this must be the house, 278. Well, thank goodness that's over," mother said.

Two days later she showed Elizabeth the headlines in the newspaper. "*Now* we can be glad, see, dear! The war's really over now."

"Is it?" Elizabeth was putting on her rubbers and did not pay much attention.

"Here," said mother. "Here's a quarter so you can go to the store and buy a flag and horn for Susie."

She went up to the corner, but slowly, because there was no one out in the streets. The quarter felt sticky inside her woollen mitt and it was hard to get it loose when she came to the store. Elizabeth asked for a flag and a horn; but the man didn't have any left.

A Week in the Country

"Jenny's got a beau! Jenny's got a beau!" Elizabeth was chanting, beneath the dining-room window. As soon as Jenny's flushed, shiny face appeared behind the lace curtain, Elizabeth made off. It was fun to tease Jenny, but dangerous too; Dickon might get too embarrassed and just go away.

Elizabeth went around to the front and sat on the fender of his Model T Ford. She rather wished Dickon hadn't come to town with his car this week, so that he and Jenny could go for a jitney ride; and take Elizabeth with them. Now that there was a street-car strike in Winnipeg many servant-girls like Jenny took their half-day off by riding around town in a jitney beside their beaux—some of them young soldiers just back from the War. Elizabeth could think of nothing nicer than riding in a jitney, unless it was going to see Charlie Chaplin or Billie Burke in the moving-pictures.

But that June there was much more excitement in store. As the weather grew warmer the news father brought home from the Free Press made the grown-ups' faces look cross and tired. People didn't laugh or joke any more about the strike. And Mother stopped going down-town. Father had seen a street-car turned right over, on Main Street. Then, one morning, all the bread and milk wagons stood idle in the yards. Elizabeth and Jenny had to walk to a citizen's depot to get milk. "General Strike" they heard people saying, horrified.

Mother decided it was time now for Elizabeth to be packed off to the country. "It's nearly the end of the term, so it won't hurt her to miss school." She turned to Jenny with her plan: "If Dickon comes to the city this week, perhaps you could have a little holiday, and take Elizabeth to your folks' farm. Dickon wouldn't mind?"

"I guess not." Jenny didn't sound very eager.

"You'd like to visit with your mother for a week or so, wouldn't you?"

"Oh, yes. I'd like real well to see them. It's just. . ."

"Just what?" Elizabeth demanded. Nosey Elizabeth.

"Oh, nothing. . . sure, I'll ask Dickon," Jenny promised.

Elizabeth jumped up and down, not knowing what it was like "in the country" but imagining all of Jenny's family to be like herself, plump and rosy with shining nut-brown hair.

They were all ready that Saturday evening when Dickon came driving along the street in his floppity Ford. The top was pushed down and it seemed to bounce at every bump. Dickon drew up with a grinding sound and climbed out carefully. He wore a shiny black suit and a red striped tie; but his face, so rough and red from the sun, did not seem to fit his clothes.

"Hello, Dickon!"

"Hello, Liz." He had that kind of a smile that made her feel warmed up.

"We're already packed, Dickon! I'll tell Jenny!"

When they started out, waving good-bye to mother, Jenny held Elizabeth between her and Dickon. She had on her sailor hat, and a motoring veil that flopped in Elizabeth's face. As soon as they were out on the prairie, on the narrow black dirt road, Dickon stopped the car. "Tuck her in the back seat. She'll rest better."

"Oh, she's all right here, aren't you, Elizabeth?" Jenny squeezed, almost poked her.

"I don't care." She felt sleepy already. "There's a rug back there."
And Dickon slid her over onto the slippery black leather. The top was
still pushed back, and she could watch the sky slowly fading from blue
and mauve into the long twilight.

It was pitch dark when she woke, hearing voices. The auto seemed to
have stopped alongside a poplar bush. Ch-rump. Ch-rump. Frogs, was
it? Overhead the sky was like a huge sieve, showering stars. Jenny's voice
came to her, murmuring from the front seat.

"No, Dickon, please. Not now, please!" And Dickon the tongue-tied
was saying, "What's the matter, Jen? You used to like a kiss."

"Not just now."

"Last year—"

"This isn't last year."

"Everything's just the same, to me."

"Well, I can't help it. I feel different. Living in the city. . ."

"I see." He was quiet, and then he came out with it, strong: "You'd
better tell me, Jenny! Is there another fellow?"

"No! There's never been anybody else but you that I've gone out with.
Honest. It's not just that, Dickon. It's just. . ."

"What?"

"Oh, I dunno. Maybe getting back to the farm. . ."

Elizabeth felt the long silence stretching between them. Then the frog
chorus arose and enveloped all the night. Dickon began to fuss with the
engine. He had to get out and crank before they were off again, speeding
into the cool country.

"Nearly home," Jenny murmured, leaning towards the back seat. But
Elizabeth pretended she was asleep.

She was awakened with a bump. No sound of the engine. Darkness
and voices. Jenny was shaking her, saying "Here she is, Bessie!" Small

warm hands seized hers. "Welcome to the farm!" Someone held a lamp over the doorway and as she entered, wrapped in encircling arms, she saw Bessie's golden brown eyes smiling into hers. Sleepily she felt her clothes being taken off. Soon she was lying in a big double bed with Bessie beside her.

"We can be downstairs in the best room," Bessie giggled, " 'cause we're both nine. The rest of the kids have to sleep up in the attic." Then Bessie's candle was blown out and they lay alone in the surrounding night.

In the morning it was Sunday. Dolly, an older sister, pounced on their bed shouting, "Sleepy heads! Sleepy heads! Come on, Bessie. It's time to make the tea."

"Tea and crackers, Sunday treat," Bessie explained. And Elizabeth forgot to say, 'I'm not allowed to have tea.' She drank hers blissfully, dribbling the cracker crumbs all over the bed.

"Never mind," Bessie said. "We'll shake 'em out and air the bedding— you and me together, eh?" Bessie was only just nine but she knew how to work. Elizabeth's fingers trembled, she struggled all day to keep up. "Come on, Liz, it's easy," Bessie encouraged, carrying a pail of water from the pump to the trough. "And then I'll show you the new piggies, and my own baby calf. Fred's his name."

Chores and play, play and chores. It seemed all part of the same life. Elizabeth, sniffing it up like some new comfort never before enjoyed, was astonished at the way Jenny complained: "All that work churning butter, ma! And in the city you just run over to the store."

"Somebody has to churn the butter," was all Mrs. Moffat said, mildly. She smiled tolerantly at Jenny, steaming over the wash-tub. "It's such hard work you have to do, mother . . . no washing machine. And it takes so darn long." Mrs. Moffat just laughed, including Elizabeth in her look. Yes, it took time. Yet the farmer found time, between his jobs, to tease the girls and to toss baby Laura high in the air.

"Ouch! Rained in your pants again. Why don't you go out in the proper place and water my seed bed, eh—you rascal?"

Laura was always wet, but nobody minded. Fun to be Laura, riding on the manure sledge, pulled by a horse. Fun to be Bessie and Dolly, starting off Monday morning for school, swinging their lunch pails. How they laughed and waved, clambering onto the school wagon, pulled slowly up and over the hill by two white horses.

Elizabeth was alone now, till nightfall. She hung around the kitchen for a while, watching Mrs. Moffat kneading dough while Jenny stood by, sighing for baker's bread "delivered right to your door." Elizabeth said nothing, just sniffed the yeasty scent and thought of the moment when the knobbly crusts would burst from the oven, filling the kitchen with fragrance. Mrs. Moffat paused long enough to put a cookie in her mouth, and a book of fairy stories into her hand. Then Elizabeth thought of the old deserted buggy beside the barn: a good place to read. She climbed up into it happily, imagining herself a fairy princess on the way to a ball. Lost in reading, it was a long time before she noticed the sun had climbed higher and was beating down upon her head. The letters danced on the dappled page, sizzling heat strafed her head.

"That'll be enough of that there sun!" the farmer called, passing by with a pail on either arm. "Come to the cool side o' the barn, girlie, and play in the dirt with Laura."

In the evening the farm came awake again. After a supper of ham and fried potatoes the children swarmed outside for games of tag, hide-and-seek, prisoner's base. The excitement of games! Elizabeth found she had to run, shrieking and panting, till her throat was as hot as a pipe-stem. She tried hard to catch the ball thrown to her; but her fingers trembled, she missed. But no one said (as her own father did), "Butter fingers!" And soon Bessie's arm was flung around her shoulder. "Let's go say goodnight to Fred." Gently they walked, arm in arm, cooling off as the prairie night wrapped itself round them.

"Let's just go tiptoe," Elizabeth dared to suggest, "and see if your calf is asleep."

"They'll all be sleeping."

When they reached the barn Bessie unfastened the bolt softly and they slipped into the gloom, into the smell of straw and manure. Dull thud of a horse's hoof, cows chewing their cud: these were the only sounds. Bessie beckoned and Elizabeth followed on tiptoe to Fred's stall. Chuckling, they stooped to rub his nose. Elizabeth tripped and nearly fell over into the stall. Right away she was petrified by a voice from the loft above: "What's that noise?" Bessie stiffened, put a finger on her lips. They they heard a man's voice murmuring, "Just the beasts below."

"It's Dickon," Bessie whispered, half giggling. She took Elizabeth's hand and they stood stock still, tight together.

Dickon spoke again. "Aw, please, Jenny, you don't have to go yet!"

They could not hear a reply, only a scuffling in the loft. Bessie could hardly hold herself in, trying not to giggle. Elizabeth was trembling, her mouth dry.

"It's a long way I walked from my place, just to go home again."

"But honestly, Dickon, Ma'll need me for the separating; I'll come back after," Jenny promised. "Now let me go, quick!"

Bessie, choking with laughter, seized Elizabeth's arm and led her on tiptoe to the barn door. "Hurry," she whispered. Elizabeth stumbled on the sill and nearly fell. They fled rocketing out the door and through the barnyard, running for dear life. In the first field they plumped into a haystack, exhausted, letting their laughter loose in the sweet prickly comfort of the hay.

When they could talk, Elizabeth choked, "Gee, what if they heard us?"

"It wouldn't matter," Bessie told her. "We kids used to peek at them last summer. Dickon lives all alone, y'know, on his Dad's old farm. He has nobody to look after him. But Ma says he's too shy to ask Jenny to marry him."

"He didn't sound shy tonight." That set them giggling again. But after they had crept home and slipped into bed Elizabeth whispered, "But why is Jenny so mean to him?"

"She's not mean!"

"She is so! She's always trying to get away from him."

"Is she? I dunno. I guess maybe she doesn't want to get married. She doesn't like the farm . . . but I do!"

"So do I. And I'd marry a farmer!" Elizabeth smiled into the dark, where she could imagine so clearly the face of Dickon: red and crusty with sandy tufted eyebrows looming above such blue eyes. Blue as . . . as cornflowers . . . sky . . . She fell asleep, still smiling.

When tomorrow came it proved to be a day for housecleaning at Dickon's farm. Jenny took the horse and gig, with Elizabeth and baby Laura up beside her. Ahead of them stretched the straight prairie road with upturned black loam stretching for miles on either side. All else was sky, blue, with puffs of cloud at the brim; and the sound of meadowlarks. It was a happy morning. Only Jenny sat heavily holding the reins, saying nothing.

Elizabeth looked up at her, hesitant; observing the rounded bloom of her cheeks, her ginger-coloured hair struggling to be free from the prim knot at the back; her brown eyes that could flash, her mouth that could pout. Why wouldn't she talk?

"Is it a long way to Dickon's house, Jenny?"

"About three miles."

"I'm glad we don't have to walk. . ." Elizabeth watched the horse's tail twitch as he clopped along. "Is it a nice house—Dickon's?"

"Nothing to get excited about." Jenny pulled the reins tighter.

"Are you going to get engaged to him, Jenny?" As there was no answer she started to say it again, more loudly; but Jenny's clouded face choked the question. They did not talk again until they reached the poplar bluff that served as gateway to Dickon's farm.

The old frame house was sagging, crouched to the earth, unpainted and curtainless. But the barn looked stronger, sturdier, as if it knew the feel of footsteps, touch of hands. While Jenny went into the house to start a fire and clean up, the two children wandered about. Around the barn there were no animals to look at. The chicken house they peered into was empty and untidy; swallows swerved in the gloom of a shed. A tightness . . . she felt a tightness in her throat. Poor Dickon, with no one to look after him! He was far off in the back field today, behind his team. He did not seem to know they were there.

"Is Dickon coming here for dinner?" Elizabeth asked, hungrily hanging around the kitchen door.

"No," said Jenny. "He takes his lunch pail out to the fields. Here, I brought some sandwiches for you and Laura."

They munched them, deep in the unshaven grass, pouring themselves drinks of water from the rusty pump. "Sp'ash, sp'ash," cried Laura, and Elizabeth obediently pumped great squirts of water over her bare feet. Then she jumped into the puddle herself, letting the mud ooze through her toes.

"Here," said Jenny, weakening. "You can take this thermos of tea to Dickon."

Elizabeth wiped her feet on the grass with alacrity, fumbled for her socks and sandals. Then she and Laura trotted off along a muddy lane, on and on through the shimmering sun to Dickon.

He was sitting in a bit of shade by a poplar bluff, eating his lunch. "Well," was all he said. "Well, well." And then, "Thanks, kiddies."

Elizabeth glowed, but she did not know what to say, standing stiffly before him. "Jenny is cleaning up for you," she offered.

"Yes," he replied. "Real nice of her, isn't it?"

"It needs cleaning," said Elizabeth.

"It does that."

"It needs a woman around, I guess." She half laughed, making it sound casual like. But he did not answer. He just looked a long way off across the flat fields. Since apparently that was all he was going to say, and he had finished his tea, Elizabeth picked up the empty thermos. "G'bye then."

"G'bye, Liz." He smiled his rare smile, his blue eyes crinkling. She went back to Jenny in a golden dream, scarcely noticing that Jenny asked no question about Dickon; nor did she look his way when the buggy, homeward bound, passed near his field.

Before Elizabeth's time was up, there was a picnic in the bush beside a creek; and a visit to a neighbouring farm. But most days curved in an arc of steady sun, black shade. In the evening, breathless after a game of tag, Elizabeth and Bessie would climb onto the field gate and swing slowly to and fro. Elizabeth always looked along the lane to see if there was anyone coming—a man in blue overalls, it might be, and a blue shirt. But Dickon never came.

"Jenny was cross as two sticks today," Elizabeth told Bessie. "I bet she's sorry she was mean to him."

"Jenny likes the city—shows, and jitneys and things," replied Bessie, who had never been there.

"And I like the country!" Elizabeth sang it out.

"I'm glad. Wisht you could always stay with us."

"So do I." Strange, she had not felt homesick yet.

But the day arrived when the farmer came driving his team home at noon, with Dickon beside him.

"Dickon!" Elizabeth ran to greet him; then hung back, shy. He really looked pleased to see her, and swung her up in his arms. Elizabeth blushed and kicked, so he set her down quickly, saying: "Why I do believe the kiddie's put on weight here!"

"You bet she has." Mr. Moffat smiled. "Too bad she has to go back."

"Go back?" Jenny echoed Elizabeth's question, suddenly appearing from the kitchen door.

"Yep. Strike's over," Dickon told them.

"They say things will be rolling again by Monday," said the farmer. " 'Bout time, too."

"Did the men win?" Jenny wanted to know.

"What's that to you? I dunno. Jones passed the word over the fence to Dickon. They've quit, that's all we know. Them ringleaders arrested."

"Well, I guess your mother will want you home again, eh, Elizabeth?" Mrs. Moffat patted her shoulder.

"Oh, I don't think Mummy would want me yet," Elizabeth asserted, casting a hopeful glance towards the farmer and his wife as they stood in the farmhouse doorway.

"Naturally Elizabeth will have to go back to her folks." Mrs. Moffat smiled firmly, putting an arm around her shoulder as they all moved inside. "Though I don't see why Jenny should have to go back so soon. She's entitled to a holiday."

They all turned to look at Jenny.

"I've had my holiday," she said.

Dickon, just inside the doorway, flushed red, moved awkwardly from one foot to the other. He managed to ask her, "Do you want me to drive you to Winnipeg tomorrow?"

"Yes, please," she said. Then she went straight to the stove and began carrying hot dishes to the kitchen table.

"Well, sit down, sit down, Dickon," urged the farmer. "Can't waste time eatin', this time of year."

On Sunday, after the heavy afternoon dinner, good-byes had to be said. Elizabeth loitered through the barnyard with Bessie; then Bessie packed her suitcase for her and tucked into it a sprig of 'everlasting'—"So you won't forget me, Elizabeth."

"Oh, thanks." She was almost choking.

"Maybe Elizabeth can come back some day," the mother said, softening and giving her a last hug. Then she was up into the front seat, between Dickon and Jenny. Everyone waved white handkerchiefs, even little Laura in her daddy's arms. Bessie ran to close the farm gate after them.

"Don't forget, Elizabeth! Don't forget!"

Elizabeth felt dry and empty. Some day, she was certain, she would return to the farm and marry Dickon and really look after him. He wasn't really so old; only twenty-four! Sitting there in the car beside him, with Jenny on the other side, she felt as if Dickon really belonged to her. She began to chatter away faster and faster, talking to him about the farm.

"You don't like the city, do you, girl?" said Dickon. He called her 'girl' now, not 'kiddie'. "Well, no more do I. No more do I." And he pressed his foot on the accelerator, hard.

Jenny said nothing, all the dusty way home.

The Uprooting

When they had returned to their second house, after the war, they saw clearly it could never be the same. Not only had it shrunk—the white clapboard that had seemed so high now looking like a doll's house set in a doll's garden—but the house possessed a secret air. The neighbours soon made known to mother what the secret was about. But even if they had not described the changes in the house, there was enough evidence, taken alone: taxis pulling up at night and unloading men; sounds of revelry; deep day silences—the house must have got used to all these, mother guessed. For the telephone would ring, at all hours: "That you, Flossie? Can I come up tonight?" Mother put down the receiver with a bang. Later she said (in front of Elizabeth) that she had thought it strange that father's steel engravings of Jove and Juno had been brought downstairs and hung in the drawing-room. Worse still, as far as Elizabeth was concerned—the blue elephant was gone. He had been a plush elephant sent by Granny—in England; and because he was so pretty he had always sat on the plate shelf, just to be looked at. Now he could never be played with. He had gone, with the tenants.

"There must have been some children here," Elizabeth argued. But no one chose to answer. From snatches of telephone conversation she gathered that "the nurse" and her mother, who had rented the house, were not really what they said they were, at all; but something queer. Probably Unitarians, Elizabeth thought.

And so the little white house had become, not father's any longer, but Someone's—nobody knew quite whose. Father blamed mother for having rented it while he was away; he wanted to sell it, and move. And then the great decision came, for him and for all of them. He was to go east! He was to have a big job to do in the newspaper world and they would live in a city called Toronto.

Leave Winnipeg! It seemed impossible. "But I can't leave Peggy!" Elizabeth said. Father just laughed. "Wait till you see the cherry trees in bloom," he promised. "And trilliums. Trilliums in Stoney Wood." Father was already re-living his youth, spent with relatives in the Ontario countryside. Enthusiasm lighted his face, he chuckled like a boy.

Cherry blossoms? She did not know. But Elizabeth had no choice. She had to go. She had to watch the little white house being dismantled; clothes and books packed; old toys thrown away. Father said they couldn't possibly take the doll's house; but Elizabeth and Susie insisted that they could, they must. The doll's house was a symbol, for them, of all their life in the larger house. Their loves and hates had entered into it; and each bit of furniture—the little coal scuttle that came from England—the tiny lamp—these objects had become as inseparable as their own hands. Mother saw this, and understood: and the doll's house was also given a ticket marked "Toronto".

It was different with people. Elizabeth, anguished, apprehended rather than reasoned that you could not take people with you. And that last morning, sitting on a suitcase on the front verandah, she felt desolate, a hollow feeling in her stomach. It was a cold spring day, nearly crocus time again. Wind blew the crows about, wherever it wished, in a grey sky: a lonely, unreal morning.

Across the street, Peggy could be seen, skipping. But oddly enough, it was not Peggy now whom she missed, whom she longed for. Peggy had changed. She stayed more at home, now that Rita had gone off to take her hospital training. And also, she played more with boys. Why, even last week Elizabeth had seen her chasing Robert, the new boy, and tripping him up—and then bending down, flinging her curls in his face, as if she were going to kiss him! This was too much for Elizabeth. She seemed to have lost Peggy, that very moment; so today it did not seem to upset her to see Peggy staying on the other side of the street, just waiting till Elizabeth's taxi came. Let her skip!

No. It wasn't her own friends Elizabeth was mourning for; nor the familiar shape of the wide street and the brown boulevard grass looking like a map, with its raised bumps of sooty, gritty snow. It wasn't the separation, even, from those beings who had watched over her like angels: Granny and Aunt Maudie. Especially Aunt Maudie, who had a way of sitting down beside you as if she knew you wanted her; and of giving you a little hug: "Well, how's my sweetness?" and putting into your hand something she had made for you. This time it was a tiny farewell sachet, smelling so keenly of lavender.

"Oh, isn't it darling!" Elizabeth smiled, nearly crying. And she remembered all the ways in which Aunt Maudie had been like a mother to her: teaching her, so patiently, to knit; to sew; to make that spicy cottage pudding with the brown sugar sauce. Aunt Maudie never gave her a book, nor paintboxes, nor musical instruments; but she made her a white eyelet embroidery dress to wear at the Sunday School concert. And at all times Aunt Maudie took the warmest interest in her doll family, and made dolls' clothes and showed Elizabeth how to make them. . . Why wasn't Aunt Maudie a mother, she wondered, suddenly; and feeling the closeness and warmth of this gentle person beside her, she burst out now with the question:

"Why didn't you ever get married, Aunt Maudie?" And Aunt Maudie smiled, without a tear in her eye. "Why, I guess I never met a man I liked well enough," she explained, simply. "I was always at home, you know; looking after your Granny."

"Oh. . . Well, if you didn't want to marry, wasn't there anything else you wanted to do, Aunt Maudie?"

And the sweet mouth smiled, the weak blue eyes behind gold-rimmed spectacles lighted up. "Why, if I could have had the training, dear—I would have liked to be a chemist. A druggist, you would call it. I was always so interested in herbs, and drugs and their uses. How to cure people.".

"A druggist!" Elizabeth looked at Aunt Maudie with increased curiosity. She could not imagine that white hair behind a counter, selling zambuk. . . perhaps she would fit in at the back, in the dispensary, fiddling about as she did in her own, terribly untidy pantry. But Aunt Maudie might so easily get the drugs mixed up, putting half-a-teaspoon of one into this saucer, and half-a-teaspoon of that into a cup. Oh, no! Elizabeth thought Aunt Maudie would have managed much better, as a mother. . . and left it at that; only realizing long afterwards that Aunt Maudie had been a mother, after all; for she had taught Elizabeth what mothering was like.

But this farewell morning Elizabeth smiled, flung her arms around Aunt Maudie's neck. "I wish you were coming with us too, Aunt Maudie."

"I wish I was, dear. I wish I was." And the gentle, work-worn hand stroked her hair, gazed into her eager eyes. "Promise me you'll be a good girl, Elizabeth? And always do what's right?"

"Yes," said Elizabeth. "I promise!" Embarrassed, she jumped up, ran down to the gate to see if the taxi was coming. That car, could it be that black car in the distance? It was! It stopped at the curb in front of the gate.

"Are you going now? Are you going?" Peggy and Frances and other girls on the street, free on their Saturday morning, came dashing over to the white house. They all wanted to help the taxi man carry valises and boxes down to the car. Then mother came out of the doorway, in a wide-brimmed hat with an ostrich feather, and carrying all kinds of little parcels and bundles. "And have you got the lunch?" asked Aunt Maudie.

And Susie ran out, carrying her rag doll; and last of all, father, turning the key in the lock though there was nothing left to lock; father, carrying a new walking-stick with a carved knob at the top.

"Goodbye, goodbye!" they called back and forth, in high childish voices, till they were all piled into the taxi and the door closed. The engine whirred, the car moved forward, backed up a side street, then tore around to a flying goodbye, goodbye to Lipton Street.

So it wasn't Peggy, nor Rita, nor Aunt Maudie, nor the street itself; nor the little white clapboard house: it was something of all these, whose loss she felt; but it was more, more than that. What she experienced was the sense of separation, the knowledge that she was no longer tied to anything; but was a human creature walking alone, with only her own legs to sustain her, her own arms to pull.

She pressed her face against the car window and saw, high overhead, scudding along amongst soft spring clouds, the deep V-wedge of the geese. She could not hear them, but she knew their song.